Never Cross A Boss

Trust Issues Book 1

Tamicka Higgins

© 2017

Disclaimer

This book contains sexually explicit content that is intended for ADULTS ONLY (+18).

Chapter 1

Kayla woke up yet again with another headache. This was starting to become a regular thing for her and, as much as she hated to admit it, having a headache when she woke up in the morning was becoming a new normal that she would come to expect. If she did not have a headache when she woke up, she wondered what the deal was – what God could be trying to tell her. As usual, the nineteen-year-old lay in bed for a little while after turning her cell phone alarm off. She looked over at her window and shook her head.

"Fuck" she said, the word practically slipping out of her mouth. From her second floor bedroom, she could see the roofs of the two houses down the street from where she lived. And there was at least a good six to seven inches of snow piled up on top of each of them – at least a few inches more than there had been last night.

Quickly, Kayla grabbed her remote and turned on the television. After a quick glance at the time, 7:05, she knew that she had at least a good thirty minutes before she had to go make sure Latrell and Linell, her younger twin brother and sister, got up and ready for school. Without even thinking about it, Kayla rolled her eyes as she scrolled through the channels until she found a cast of newscasters and stopped. There was no doubt in her mind that her mother probably did not come home last night. In fact, since she had basically stopped coming home to be a mother who actually did what she was supposed to do, Kayla's headaches had begun. It was depressing to think about, yet it was her reality.

Kayla watched the news, waiting to see if there were school cancellations. Part of her wished that Latrell and Linell would not have to go to school today. However, another part of her wished that they did. As good as lying back down in the bed and going back to sleep sounded to her, she would rather that they go to school than for her to have to deal with them all day. There was just no telling when her mother would come walking through the door from whatever nigga's place she was at. This was all getting to be just too much.

The names of schools and churches, as well as some office buildings in town that were further out in rural areas, rolled across the bottom of the screen as the newscasters talked about something or another. Kayla watched, waiting for the schools that started with the letter 'I' to roll by – in search of Indianapolis Public Schools. In minutes, the verdict was in. Indianapolis Public School: NO DELAYS rolled across the bottom of the screen. Kayla sighed and pushed her head back into her pillow then turned, looking at the snowy roofs of the two houses next door. She just hoped that the salt trucks were out last night and the main streets were at least decently cleared. Indianapolis was pretty good about that so she knew that she could relax about it all and just be sure that she drove her mother's car carefully.

Just then, Kayla felt her phone vibrated. At first, she assumed it was her phone alarm starting to go off again. When she picked up her phone and looked, she saw that it was a text message from her boo, Marcus. A smile popped onto her face as she opened it.

Marcus: Wassup Bae?

Kayla responded: Just woke up…U?

While Kayla waited for a response from Marcus, she picked the remote up and turned the television off. Once again, her bedroom was completely silent as the sun was slowly rising in the east. Her life was just not getting any better staying with her mother. Kayla thought about how her boyfriend, Marcus, had been talking to her about moving away from Indianapolis. As good as doing something like that sounded in discussion, she knew that if she did her bother and sister's life would probably not be the same. Ever since her mother and father had split up some years ago, her mother had just not been the same. Suddenly, Kayla felt more like a mother to her brother and sister than their actual mother was. At first, it was nice. In all reality, she did not mind helping to take care of them and taking them places and stuff. However, after a while, her own life began to suffer. She and Marcus, who had known each other since she was freshman in high school and he was a sophomore, weren't able to spend as much time together as they were used to. There were times that Kayla would have to cancel what the two of them were doing because her mother was not around to do whatever her little brother and sister needed. In so many ways, it went from being fun to aggravating and just so damn unpredictable.

Kayla's phone vibrated. Quickly, she picked it up and opened the text message from Marcus: Shit. Layin' in bed with a hard-on.

A giggle slipped out of Kayla's mouth. There had been a handful of nights where Kayla spent the night over at Marcus' place. Last night was supposed to be one of those nights. However, that all changed when her mother text messaged her saying that she didn't know when she would be home and asking if Kayla could make sure that Latrell and Linell get something to eat before they go to bed.

Marcus: No response, huh?

Kayla: Was just thinkin.

Marcus: Bout?

Kayla: Nothin.'

Within a few seconds, a picture message popped up from Marcus. When Kayla opened the message, she found that it was a picture of Marcus' hard dick tenting in his gray boxer briefs as he lay in bed. Kayla laughed a little and shook her head. A couple more seconds passed and a message popped up from Marcus: Is this what you was thinkin' bout.

Kayla: Nigga, shut up. It's too early for all that. Plus, you know I ain't supposed to see shit like that. I'mma lady.

Marcus: Ha! It don't be too early for that when you spend the night over here. And ain't nothin' wrong with a lady thinking about some dick.

Kayla: ROFL Marcus stop.

Marcus: When you comin' through? Ur mama come home or not?

Kayla started to respond to Marcus' text message when she realized that she really didn't know. Looking at the time, she slid out of her bed quickly and walked over to her bedroom door. When she opened it, semi-cold air rushed in and collided with her 5'3 body. Dressed in a white t-shirt and some cute pink pajama pants, Kayla quickly walked down the hallway. She paused at her mother's bedroom door, trying to see if she could hear her snoring. When she didn't hear anything, she softly opened the door and stepped inside. Nothing was changed and her mother was not there. A deep sigh slipped out of Kayla's mouth, now realizing that it was a definite thing that she would be going out into the snow to get her brother and sister to school. She turned around and went right back to her bedroom.

Not even getting back into her bedroom, Kayla grabbed her phone and responded to Marcus: I just checked. That bitch ain't here again.

Marcus: Damn.

Kayla responded, shaking her head: Yeah. I'mma have to take them to school today.

Marcus: Bet. Come through when you drop them off. Let me get in that pussy.

Kayla smiled: Nigga, whatever.

Marcus: I'll be up and waiting for you. Don't take too long.

Kayla shook her head as she dropped her phone back onto the bed and stretched. She then walked over to her window and looked down outside. A car passed by on the street, not really seeming to be going all that slow. Kayla took a closer look at the street and knew that she could make it the couple of blocks down to 25th Street and be alright. Closing her blinds, Kayla got into her strong mood and knew that she would just have to keep things moving. Since she didn't get to spend last night with Marcus, she saw no reason she wouldn't stop by and spend a little time with him after she dropped her brother and sister off at school. Hell, at this point, Marcus was turning out to be Kayla's only piece of stability in a world that seemed to be on her shoulders 24/7.

Kayla walked to Latrell and Linell's bedroom and turned the light on.

"Wake up, wake up," she announced. "Time to get ready for school. Get up, y'all. C'mon y'all."

Slowly but surely, Kayla watched as her nine-year-old brother and sister climbed out of their beds. Both of them were sleepy eyed, to be expected.

"Y'all figure out who gon' shower first while I'm cookin," Kayla told them. "And neither one of y'all betta not get back in either of them beds and go back to sleep while I'm down stairs. It snowed again so we ain't got time for no bullshit."

On that note, Kayla walked out of the room and headed downstairs. Her mother, Rolanda, had never been the kind of woman to wake up in the morning and cook breakfast for her children. Since that was something that Kayla kind of always wanted when she was a little girl, she had decided a long time ago that once she had children, she would be that mother that got up them up in the morning and cooked them a little something to eat on their way into school. Little did she know when she first made that promise to herself that she would be doing it a lot sooner than she thought.

The first floor of the double they lived in was its usual tidiness. No matter how her mother lived, she always made it a priority to keep her placing looking nice. She didn't believe that children were a valid excuse for having a house that was anything less than what you wanted. In the living room, which was the room where the front door is, there was a large entertainment system with large television commanding your attention as soon as anybody walked in the room. Setting at the base of the staircase was a nice cabinet that had come from Kayla's grandmother. On top of it, was a fish tank with pictures sitting to both of its sides.

Kayla slid through the dining room, around a cherry oak dining set and into the kitchen. When Kayla flipped the kitchen light on, the light practically bounced off of the stainless steel appliances. Quickly, Kayla began getting pans out and started to make French toast, eggs, and a couple strips of bacon for her brother and sister. She looked in the refrigerator and found herself in luck: there was enough orange juice left to where they wouldn't have to drink water. Right then, she made a mental note to herself to ask her mother when she could take the food stamp card and go get some groceries. Keeping the house stocked up with food had basically become Kayla's responsibility at this point, and there were times it got so tiresome asking her mother for the food stamp card. It got even harder when she wasn't around.

Kayla made her sister and brother their plates and set them in front of two chairs at the small kitchen table, wedged in the corner of the kitchen. Just as she was going upstairs to make sure that things were going smoothly with her brother and sister, the two of them were coming downstairs.

"Good deal," Kayla said, happy to see that they hadn't gotten back in the bed and fallen asleep. "Y'all breakfast is sitting in there on the table. Make sure y'all get y'all backpacks and stuff before we leave."

"What you make to eat?" Latrell asked. Out of the two of them, Latrell liked it more when his older sister woke them up and took them to school. Whatever she would make for them to eat would always be better than the food they could get at school during breakfast. Plus, there were times, especially when their mama was taking them to school, that they would not get there in time to go to breakfast. On top of that, she never made breakfast. With Kayla, they got to eat breakfast at home and if they were still hungry, they would always get to school in time to go to breakfast in the cafeteria if they wanted. If they weren't hungry, they could hang out with their friends out in the hallway until it was time to go to class.

"Just go on in there and see," Kayla answered as she headed upstairs to get her own self ready. "It ain't nothin' spectacular or nothin."

When Kayla got to her bedroom, she grabbed a towel, some clean clothes – nothing too cute or anything – and headed to the bathroom. She turned on the shower and began to undress. As she did, however, she could not help that with age, she was only getting better looking. There were times that she would look at herself in the mirror and be in disbelief at the young woman she was turning out to be. It was almost like karma for all the people who used to talk shit about her in middle school and in her early years of high school, when she was just thin without much shape to speak of at all.

Now, all that had changed. Now? Now, she had a body that so many women would kill for and she could not lie to herself and say that she did not cherish it. At a little over five feet, she weighed 130 pounds and was thick in just all the right places. Her waist curved out to some nice hips, and those led down to thick thighs that jiggled ever so slightly when she walked. Her chest had even filled out, going from just an A when she was maybe a freshman to a full-blown C-cup by the time she graduated in the spring of last year. Kayla had even changed up her entire approach to how she took care of her hair. Back when she was younger, she would always have some sort of weave going. In many ways, this was only because she was so heavily influenced by her mother. Hell, she had lived with that woman her entire life and could probably count on one hand the number of times she had seen her real hair. Kayla had decided some years back that she wanted to be different. When she was sixteen or seventeen years old, she stopped using weave altogether and grew her own hair out. Now, she had thick black hair that was real and lay on her shoulders. No dye, very little chemicals. As Kayla was pulling it up into her shower cap, she ran her hands through it and smiled. Having such good, long hair made her feel so beautiful. On top of it making her feel better, Marcus loved to run his hands through it. And Kayla always believed the old saying that a man running his hands through a woman's hair was way to make it grow more. Plus, it was so soothing.

Kayla took a quick, but thorough shower and hopped out. After drying off and sliding into her clothes, she hurried to her bedroom. There, she noticed her phone was blinking. It was a text message from Marcus – a picture message. "What this nigga send me again?" Kayla asked herself out loud as she shook her head and opened the text message. Again, it was a dick picture from Marcus with a smiling emoji underneath. Kayla shook her head and chuckled as she responded: Nigga, it is too early for all this.

Just as Kayla was grabbing her purse and coat, her phone vibrated again. Marcus: No it ain't. Hurry up and get that pussy over here before I get angry.

Kayla, thinking back to one of Marcus' responses from earlier, responded: Ha! And I'm supposed to care that you angry or somethin?

Within seconds, Marcus responded: You will. ☺

Kayla rolled her eyes and shook her head as she made sure she had everything she needed, turned her bedroom light off, and headed back downstairs. Latrell and Linell were in the kitchen, finishing up their breakfast as they argued about which Chris Brown song was better.

"Hurry up y'all," Kayla told them. "Y'all know that it snowed outside and we might need some extra time to get up there. Stop foolin' round."

Latrell snickered and looked across the table at his twin sister. "You know what that means," he said, sarcastically.

Linell nodded, smiling. "Hmm, hmm," she said.

Just then, Kayla's neck snapped back and her eyes fell onto her brown-skined brother and sister. She smiled, finding it so cute how the two of them had their own little bond going. On the other hand, there were moments like these were it kind of sucked for her being the outsider.

"And what is that supposed to mean?" Kayla asked.

"Nothing," Latrell said, going back to chewing a piece of bacon. "Nothing at all."

"So why you say you know what that means when I told y'all that you betta hurry up so we can get going?" Kayla asked.

The nine year olds looked up at their older sister and smiled. Kayla opened her eyes wider, looking them both in the eyes and letting them know that she wanted an answer. "Well?" she asked.

"Is Marcus coming over when you drop us off at school?" Latrell asked.

While the plan was not for Marcus to come over after she dropped them off, Kayla could not help but to blush a little bit. Here were these two nine year olds that were smart enough to figure out exactly what was up. Out of instinct, Kayla just started to shake her head. "Hell naw," she said. "What makes you say that?"

"Because," Linell said. "Y'all was supposed to be hanging out last night but I remember when you were on the phone saying that you wouldn't be able to go over there because Mama said she wasn't coming home."

"Damn," Kayla said, wanting to practically burst into laughter. "Why you all in my business like that?"

Latrell looked up at his sister and waved his finger side to side. "You shouldn't have your business out there like that."

Kayla almost gagged, thinking of how these kids were growing up just a little too fast and hearing some grown folk things that they just shouldn't be hearing. "Oh no you didn't," she said, gently slapping her brother upside his head.

"Owe," Latrell said, doing the most. "Don't hit me like that. Mister John came to the school and told us that was domestic violence."

"And it affects men, too," Linell said, adding her own two cents to the mix.

Just then, Kayla squinted her eyes at Latrell and Linell. She pointed at the food setting in front of them. "Hurry up and domestic violence that food right on up so we can get outta here," Kayla said, leaving the kitchen.

As she walked to the front room, she could hear the two of them snickering and talking amongst themselves in the kitchen. In the few minutes that she would be waiting on them to finish their breakfast, she decided to watch the news a little. Kayla normally didn't watch the news all the much. However, since she was starting to be somewhat the responsible caregiver for these two little kids, she had gotten into a habit of watching just to see if there was anything going on in the city or out on the roads that she should be aware of. Just as the commercials were going off and the news was coming back on, the front door swung open. Cold, winter air rushed inside the living room as Kayla's mother Rolanda came hurrying in.

"Damn, it's cold out there," Rolanda said.

Kayla rolled her eyes and put her attention back onto the television screen. "Good morning, Mama."

Instantly sensing a little attitude, Rolanda turned around and looked her daughter Kayla up and down. "And what is your problem?"

Kayla looked at her mother, noticing how she was half-assed put together. Her hair, which she had just gotten done not more than three days ago, was looking somewhat untamed. Kayla gave her the benefit of the doubt and figured that it could have been a combination of sleeping on it wherever she was, the wind, and the snow. In the back of her mind, however, Kayla figured that none of those were the real reason her mother's head was looking so unpresentable. Furthermore, her entire appearance looked like she had just been getting some dick somewhere. Her sweater was wrinkled and halfway pulled down over her very shapely lower body. Her red pants were so tight they looked like another layer of skin, pronouncing the dimples in her thighs. Her makeup was just gone at this point.

"I ain't say I had no problem," Kayla said. "I was just saying good morning. How was your evening?"

Rolanda had had enough of her daughter's mouth lately. She understood that she was a young woman now and not a little girl. However, she still was her child and lived under her roof. There were certain things that she just could not slide. On top of all that, her head was killing her right then. She had only had a few hours of sleep over at Kevin's place before she woke up to use the bathroom and decided to just go on and carry her ass home.

"My evening was fine, if you must know," Rolanda said as she got herself together from coming in out of the cold. "I'm not sure I'm liking this tone you're taking with me right now, Kayla."

Just then, Kayla rolled her eyes then tossed the remote back onto the couch. Once she'd seen that nothing had changed in terms of her day, whatever her mother was saying to her was irrelevant at that moment.

"Kayla?" Rolanda said, never liking when she was ignored. "Little bitch, what the fuck is your fuckin' problem?"

"Latrell, Linell!" Kayla announced heading into the dining room and grab both her brother's and sister's coats. "Come on, y'all, so we can get going. Come on and hurry up, y'all!"

"Kayla?" Rolanda said, again. "I know you hear me talking to you."

Kayla turned and looked at her mother, still standing in the living room, just to the side of the television. The older Kayla got, and especially since she graduated and had more time at home compared to when she was in school, the less she could really stand to be around her mother. Everything about her was just a big turn off. To Kayla, in fact, it was quickly starting to feel like she was talking to someone that was in the same age group as her. And she just did not like that, especially when her mother would get into her bratty ways. To Kayla, that shit was just not cute.

"Damn," Kayla said, feeling frustrated that her mother would come walking through the door at the last minute like this and trying to get her in her shit. "What, Mama? What?"

"What is the attitude about?" Rolanda asked again.

"I told you," Kayla said. "I ain't got no attitude. I don't even know why you try'na come in right after the crack of dawn and act like you try'na be a mother for all of ten minutes today. Damn, Mama. That shit ain't cute."

Rolanda was appalled at what she was hearing out of Kayla's mouth.

"Kayla," Rolanda said. "Little bitch, I think you ought to be showing me a little more respect than that. I mean, after all, look around." Rolanda's arms were now waiving around as she pointed at different pieces of furniture and the entertainment system. "I keep a roof over your head and shit and when I wanna go out and have a little fun, I come home to you giving me the cold shoulder and shit like I done did you wrong or something. If you don't like having to do something around here, why the fuck you don't just move out and go stay with that nigga, whatever his name is, and do whatever he need you to do for you to get him to take care of you. You grown now, and I guess that's why you got this shitty attitude. But I'm lettin' you know. I ain't feelin' this shit and I definitely am not the one. I ain't even had that much sleep."

"Ain't that a shame," Kayla said, rolling her eyes and sounding sarcastic in her delivery. "I guess I got a little bit of sleep. I knew I'd have to get up and play mommy. Some of us can't say the same."

Just then, Latrell and Linell came running into the dining room. They approached Kayla, who handed each of them their coat. They started to slide into them as they picked up on what was going on between their mother and their older sister. Instantly, the two nine year olds could feel the tension in the room. It was oh so obvious.

"Play mommy," Rolanda said, shaking her head. "Girl, you really done got that head blown up. Thinking you really up in her doin' something, huh? Is that what the fuck is goin' through your mind? Look here, Kayla. Listen up, little girl. You ain't did shit. Ever since that nigga that is your no good daddy left, you've had the best life I can provide to you and this is the thanks I get."

Kayla helped Latrell zip his coat all the way up to his neck. "I see you still a little messed up from last night, huh?" Kayla said, shaking her head. "I damn sure was not givin' you any thanks, Rolanda."

"Girl, what has gotten into you?" Rolanda asked as she marched into the dining room. In the light and much closer than when she'd come in from outside, Kayla could see the bags under her mother's eyes. It was very obviously she had probably been up drinking and smoking, somewhere, for several hours then had a nap before rushing home like a teenage girl who stayed out passed her curfew.

"Mama, whatever," Kayla said, just wanting her mother to walk away or go do something – anything – with herself and get the hell out of her face. "It's too early for this," Kayla said in a very definitive tone. "And, unlike a certain chill chick I know, I got to get my little brother and sister to school." Just then, Kayla turned up and looked at her mother, looking dead into her eyes. "You know you wasn't gon' do it," she said. "Anytime you supposed to get them up and take them to school, they wind up being late or missing the first couple of hours and we start getting them calls from the school."

"Kayla," Rolanda said. "You not gon' be talkin' to me like I'm some bad mother or something, you hear me? That's exactly why I came home when I did." At this point, Rolanda was lying and she knew it. She just could not allow her grown daughter who lived in her house to talk to her any old kind of way. There were certain things that she just would not put up with. "I mean, if you got that much of a problem doin' a little somethin' around here, you can take your grown self and get to steppin' right on out the door. Get a fuckin' job and get your own place, or go move in with that nigga you call a boyfriend. I don't give a fuck what you do, but I can tell you this. You won't be talkin' to me any old kind of way, I don't care how old and grown you get." Just then, Rolanda felt herself getting thirsty. She had smoked a couple of blunts with Kevin before the two of them passed out last night. She went to sleep with cotton mouth and woke up with at as well. And it was killing her to keep talking like that with Kayla without getting something to drink. "Go stay with that nigga, whatever his name is. Maybe he'll let you sit up and do nothing. You not gon' talk to me like this, I can tell you that."

Kayla looked down into her siblings eyes, finding their eyes locked on hers and practically coming close to swelling with tears. This was not the first time that the two nine year olds had seen their older sister Kayla getting in their mother's shit. Furthermore, it would not be the last. Regardless, they hated when it happen, especially if everything else was going nicely. It always put Kayla in a bad mood.

"Y'all ready?" Kayla asked, smiling. "Come on. I gotta get y'all to school. And we gotta let the car warm up a little bit. Did y'all get enough to eat?"

The two of them nodded.

"Good deal," Kayla said. "Grab your book bags and let's go."

Just then, Latrell and Linell each grabbed their backpacks off of the couch pressed against the wall in the living room and headed toward the door.

"And now you takin' my spare car to take them to school, huh?" Rolanda asked. It was very clear to Kayla that her mother's tone was very condescending. To say the least, it really grinded her gears that she had to deal with her mother's nasty attitude when she was the one getting up to do what her mother ought to be doing.

"Girl, bye," Kayla said, just wanting to move on and get out of the door.

Kayla followed Latrell and Linell to the front door. Just as they pulled the door open and cold wind rushed into the living room, Kayla could hear her mother talking yet again from the doorway to the kitchen.

"And come right back with my car and shit," Rolanda said. "Since I ain't shit, ain't no reason for you to be using my car to get anywhere else. I'll see you in an hour."

"Mama, whatever," Kayla said. Just then, she stepped out onto the front poor and shut the door behind her. Those kinds of moments were the kinds of moments where Kayla really wished it was the last time closing the door behind. She wished it was the last time that she would have to deal with her mother walking through the door with her usual shitty demeanor. However, Kayla was just not having the best of luck with getting a job, and she really was not all that turned on by the idea of going back to school. In so many ways, high school had sort of fried her brain and she at least needed a couple of years off before she even considered doing something like that.

While Kayla waited in the car with Latrell and Linell, waiting for her mother's car to warm up after taking a short broom out of the back and sweeping the several inches of snow off of the windows, all she could think about was Marcus. Lately, she felt like everything was really starting to get serious with Marcus. However, a couple of weeks ago, when the two of them were chilling over at his place, Kayla made it a point to bring up moving in together. To say the least, Marcus just did not seem all that turned on by the idea. In fact, he was so indifferent to it that talking about it didn't even happen. Rather, the topic of the conversation changed and next thing Kayla knew, she was still back at square one – a square where she was basically a prisoner in her mother's house while also doing her job as a mother.

Feeling a little angry about her mother coming in and trying to start some shit so early in the morning, Kayla went ahead and held her head high. She knew, inside and out, that she was not a dumb chick. She knew that even though her current situation was not ideal, it would only be temporary. Plus, she also thought on the bright side. She knew deep down that she would probably feel guilty if she did move out and leave her brother and sister to fend for themselves when it came to Mama. The older she got, the less fucks she gave. And it was increasingly becoming obvious.

Kayla drove Latrell and Linell toward School 42, which sat at the corner of 25th Street and Rader Street. The drive was only about a mile and a half. However, with the snow, Kayla had to be sure to take it slow, particularly at the corners. Yes, the main streets, like Martin Luther King Jr., were cleared, but the side streets were a slushy mess. Kayla felt so lucky that the temperature was not lower, or else the slush would have frozen over to some nasty ice.

"Kayla, what were you and mama arguing about?" Linell asked.

Kayla looked at Linell in the reflection of the rearview mirror. She smiled, loving how her little sister was always so caring. At the same time, though, she hated how she was such an intelligent, yet inquisitive, girl to only be nine years old. Kayla shook her head.

"Nothing," Kayla answered. "You know how Mama be acting."

"Was she drunk and high, again?" Latrell came out and asked.

Just then, Kayla shook her head. She hated that her younger brother and sister could pick up on something like that. It always made her so uncomfortable to have to talk about that kind of stuff with them. However, even to them at nine years old, it was becoming obvious. There were times that their mother Rolanda would come walking through the door as if she was in a little bit of pain. Other times, she would come walking through the door with eyes that were practically blood shot red – not to mention the times she came home and passed out on the living room couch and wreaked of alcohol even when you just walked by her.

"Look, don't y'all worry about all that," Kayla said. "Y'all just kids and shit. Ain't no point in worrying about whatever Mama was talkin' bout. Plus, y'all know how she be trippin'.

She was just tired and not really feelin' right. Y'all know she gon be actin' totally different when you see her later on today, after she done passed out finally and got some sleep. Don't trip over her. Just worry about school."

Kayla pulled up on the side of School 42, waiving at the security guard who was standing by the door as kids walked from their parents' vehicles to the doors of the school. He was a tall, somewhat chubby dude that had a really country boy kind of smile about him. At first, Kayla hadn't even noticed him. However, after some months of her starting to basically play mommy, she noticed how hard he would be looking her way. After a while, he would start to smile then waive. Now it was the kind of thing where the two of them would waive and smile when they saw each other in the morning, but nothing else.

Kayla said bye to Latrell and Linell as they climbed out of the car and made their way toward the doors to the school. Once they were inside, the security guard waived again and Kayla waived back. She pulled off, hyperventilating. Thoughts about what her mother had come home saying to her and how she was starting shit began to come through her mind again. Just as she came to a stop at a corner a block or so down from the school, she could feel her phone vibrating in her pocket. Instantly, she began smiling. She already knew that it would be Marcus.

"This nigga bet 'not have sent another dick pic," Kayla said, as she shook her head and dug her cell phone out of her coat pocket. After quickly checking her rearview mirror to see if any cars were coming behind her, and seeing that the street was clear, she opened the text message.

Marcus: You forget about a nigga, huh?

Kayla giggled, shaking her head. Just as she began to type out a reply to Marcus' message, she decided that she would go ahead and just call.

"Hello?" Marcus answered, clearly sounding as if he was still lying in bed.

"Nigga, don't be answering like you pullin' yourself out of deep sleep," Kayla said, wanting to laugh. "You already know that you been up for at least a good hour and a half."

Marcus chuckled, his deep voice sounding so smooth through the phone. "You don't know that," Marcus said, clearly sounding as if he was purposely trying to sound snappy. "It ain't like you was layin' up with a nigga last night or anything, so how you know?"

Kayla sighed and shook her head. "Marcus, don't even get me started on that shit," she said. "You not gon' believe what happened this morning when I was gettin' Latrell and Linell ready for school."

"Hold up," Marcus said, halting the conversation. "Where you at?"

"Over off Martin Luther King, why?" Kayla answered.

"I wasn't try'na talk to you over the phone," Marcus said. "I wanna see you and touch you....and feel you."

"Damn, nigga," Kayla said, smiling. "You always horny and shit, ain't you?"

Marcus chuckled. "When I'm talkin' to you," he answered.

"Nigga, please," Kayla said. "Stop with the romantic shit. I'm on my way."

"Good," Marcus said. "I got a blunt already waiting."

"Aight, aight," Kayla said, now seeing that a car was pulling up on her bumper. "I'll be over there in like twenty minutes or so."

"Okay, okay," Marcus said. "Be careful," he added.

Kayla almost blushed at hearing that – at hearing the very words she knew that her own mother should have been telling her just twenty minutes earlier when she and her brother and sister were walking out the door.

***

Marcus had had his own place for a minute, maybe like a year and half or so. In fact, ever since he hit eighteen years old, as a senior in high school, he moved out of his mother's house. At first, he had a roommate then he found a place he was cool with to have on his own. He was already growing into his own man, and making some real money by moving that work out in the streets. Last thing he needed was his mother and father breathing down his neck. They were always asking so many questions. The way they tried to fill in gaps in Marcus' story and his schedule just drove him crazy. On top of all that, Marcus knew that if he wanted things to go rather smoothly with Kayla, it would probably just be better that he just stayed out on his own.

Marcus stayed on the other side of Naptown, in some apartments off of 34th and Shadeland. They were not among the best places in the city to live; however, Kayla sure didn't mind going to chill over there. Everything was always so on chill mode, at to make things better she really enjoyed the time she spent with Marcus. He always knew how to talk to her about everything, and today would probably be no different. The entire thirty minutes that it took Kayla to drive from the 30th and Martin Luther King area, all the way out Interstate 70 to the Shadeland exit, there was this feeling building up inside of her. It ate away at her soul, letting her know that she was ready to let it off her chest.

Kayla pulled into a parking spot outside of Marcus apartment and walked up to the door. Just as she got to the door and knocked, it swung up. She stepped inside.

"I know you ain't lost the key I gave you to a nigga's place, have you," Marcus said.

Kayla pushed the door shut behind her, shaking a little to knock off the chill in her body from being out in the cold. Just as she turned around to greet Marcus, she could feel his lips pressing into her own. After a short kiss, the two broke away and smiled at one another while looking into the other's eyes. Marcus, tall and lean with dark skin and tattoos up and down his left arm, was dressed in just gray sweatpants. In the face, throughout his years in school, Marcus had always been told that he looked like a taller, more rugged version of Ray J. While Kayla did not always agree with that kind of statement, at the least Marcus was definitely very handsome. She smiled, feeling extremely happy to be at his place and to finally get to spend a little time with him.

"Well, good morning," she said, smiling.

"Good morning," Marcus said, smiling back. "So, like a nigga said, I know you ain't lost the key to my shit, have you?"

"Nigga, please," Kayla said, taking her keys out of her pocket. "You know I ain't done no shit like that. I got the key." She sat her keys on his little kitchen table. "You know it's too cold and snowy and shit for me to be outside and fumbling with them keys while I try to figure out what keys is yours."

Marcus squinted his eyes, nodding his head. "Hmm, hmm," he said and smiled. Just then, he grabbed Kayla by her tight waist, lowering his hand to just where her lower back met with the upper area of her behind. He kissed her softly before pulling away. "I got that blunt if you wanna smoke."

"Hell yeah," Kayla said, liking how she and Marcus had always clicked.

"How long can you stay?" Marcus asked as Kayla followed him into the living room. They plopped down onto his beige couch, side by side, while Marcus grabbed what he called his Smoke Box – a little brown suede box – off of the coffee table.

"What you mean how long can I stay?" Kayla snapped back, not really understanding the question. "You make it sound like I'm a kid or some shit."

"No," Marcus said, starting to explain. "I was asking because I ain't know if you would have to take the kiddos lunch up to Forty-two or not." He chuckled at the end of his sentence.

Kayla slapped Marcus's leg, smiling and shaking her head. "Ha ha," she said, sarcastically. "Very funny. But look, let me tell you 'bout this morning."

"Oh God," Marcus said, smiling. "Here we go with this shit again."

"Listen, listen," Kayla said.

Listening, Marcus checked over the blunt, then started to light it.

"So, I'm up this morning getting them ready for school and shit," Kayla said. "And guess who come walkin' through the door: my mama."

"Word?" Marcus said. "Wait a second, and what time was this."

"Fuck if I know," Kayla answered, shrugging her shoulders. "It was only like a hour ago, if that. So, anyway, she come walking through the door and right off the bat, she get right to trying to start shit with me."

"Here," Marcus said, handing the blunt to his girl. "Hit this shit." Smoke billowed out of his nostrils as he nodded, signifying that what they were smoking was some good shit. "You'll feel better. I can tell you stressed."

Taking a break from her story for just a second, Kayla felt like she had to let Marcus know something. "You know I'm not supposed to be smoking this shit," Kayla said.

"And why is that?" Marcus asked, smiling. "You the one that got a nigga into smoking."

"Nigga, don't start that shit," Kayla said. "But you know I ain't supposed to be smoking cause I'm try'na find a job and shit."

"Look," Marcus said, looking dead into Kayla's eyes. "You know I wouldn't make you do shit you don't wanna do. I just ain't that kind of nigga. Give the blunt back to me then if you not gon' smoke. I smoke it all, it ain't no problem."

Just as Marcus reached for the blunt, Kayla pulled back and smiled. "I ain't say I ain't gon smoke it, though," she said. "I was just letting you know where I stand."

Kayla hit the blunt a couple of times then handed it back to Marcus.

"You always try'na act funny and shit with a nigga," Marcus said as he took the blunt back. "You know you was gon' smoke that shit. And if you get called for a job soon, all you gon' do is use somebody piss and go up in there to pass. Just like you did when you was workin' downtown."

"Whatever," Kayla said, rolling her eyes. At times, she hated how well Marcus knew her. It was crazy how well the two of them got on. In fact, even though she'd had a couple of boyfriends before Marcus, there was something about Marcus that really since the day the two of them started talking, that they clicked. "So, anyway, back to what I was saying," Kayla went on explaining. "So, yeah, she come walking through the door right before I'm bout to help Latrell and Linell get their coats on. As usual, you can tell that she don't just came from fucking around all night. Probably had a couple hours of sleep after passing out on that nigga Kevin's couch or some shit.

She ain't have red eyes and shit this time, but I could tell that she was cranky and shit. Straight from the jump, she come in asking me why I got a attitude. Mind you, it like the fuckin' crack of dawn and I'm up doin' her job and shit."

"That's just what I was thinking," Marcus said. "Why the fuck she come this late in the game when she know her kids gotta be up for school and shit and basically already out the door."

"Cause she stupid," Kayla said, coming across as sounding very cold. "You know how my mama is, Marcus. Ever since her and daddy broke up, and really before if you ask me, it's like she done started to have one of them…what do you call it?"

"Mid-life crisis or some shit?" Marcus asked.

Kayla smacked her hands together just before Marcus was handing the blunt back to her. "Or some shit," she said. "Fuck if I know. Long story short, she come walkin' through the door after I done got her kids up and ready and even fed they asses breakfast and shit and she start talkin' to me about my attitude. I swear, baby." Here, Kayla head was starting to shake as she fought of the urge to tear up. "I don't know how much more of her shit I can take. She was tellin' me that I can move out and shit if I don't wanna do nothing around the house and how I live in her house and all that crap. That still don't make it right, though, that she got a couple of nine year olds who are probably wondering why their mother is staying out later and more often than their nineteen year old sister. I mean, damn. I can't even live my fuckin' life as a young woman without having to take care of some kids that ain't even my kids to begin with."

Marcus sighed, smiling every so slightly as he looked at Kayla. "Yeah," he said, nodding his head.

Kayla looked at Marcus, quickly taking in the sleepy grin on his face. "Nigga, what the fuck you thinkin' bout?" she asked.

Marcus chuckled, taking the blunt back from Kayla and hitting it quickly. "Just how you get to being so worked up and shit," he answered.

"Nigga, this shit ain't funny," Kayla said.

Marcus shrugged. "I ain't say it was funny," he said. "You did. It's just…cute..HeHe… How yo mama get you all worked up and shit."

"You just don't know what the fuck I be over there goin' through," Kayla explained.

"I can imagine," Marcus said, looking Kayla's body up and down, taking in the way her ass expanded away from her body with how she was sitting on the couch not too far from him.

"Naw you can't," Kayla said. "That shit get to me so damn bad. And today, she was talkin' bout come right back with her car."

"Oh?" Marcus said. "So you was just stopping through then?"

"Hell naw," Kayla said, shaking her head. "She gon' get her fuckin' car back when I fuckin' feel like it. Ain't no point in me rushin' back over there to her drunk, high ass no way."

Just then, Marcus leaned in and wrapped his arm around Kayla's waist. "Shit," he said. "Chill over here all day. You know you want to."

"Nigga, you don't know that."

Kayla and Marcus spent the next several minutes chit chatting about this and that while they finished smoking the blunt. Once the blunt had gotten too small to hold without burning the tips of his fingers, Marcus put it into an ashtray. Now, his focus and undivided attention was put onto Kayla. She was looking so good to him that he really had to restrain himself and control his hands. His head was slowly feeling lighter and lighter as he could not help but to smile and chuckle at how worked up she got over certain things. There was no doubt in his mind that all Kayla needed was some good dick to calm down. She was always getting worked up over stuff and just needed some deep dicking to finally chill out.

Once the conversation fell flat and there was this almost awkward silence Marcus's living room, Kayla noticed and looked over at him.

"Why you not talkin' all of the sudden?" she asked.

Marcus smiled and nodded. "You know," he answered, tapping on his lap.

Kayla looked down and smiled, noticing how there was a growing bulge in Marcus's sweatpants. She leaned in and kissed him, placing her hand on his manhood.

"Oh, do I?" she asked, in a seductive way. "Is that why you want me over here?"

Marcus smiled and chuckled. "No," he answered. "But I know that's why you came."

Kayla rolled her eyes and smiled while gripping Marcus' manhood.

"Why you teasin' a nigga?" Marcus asked. "Take that shit out like you always do. Stop playin." At the end of his sentence, he leaned forward and smacked Kayla's round ass. "You know you want to see him, so I don't even know why you playin'."

"Nigga, you betta calm down," Kayla said.

"Ha," Marcus said, sarcastically. "I know if I look through that phone, I'll find some pictures of this dick in there that you probably been lookin' at before you go to bed and shit."

"The only pictures I got of your dick in my phone would be from you sending them to me and shit, without me even requesting them," Kayla said.

Marcus placed his hand on the top of Kayla head and gently rubbed. Kayla's eyes rolled, as she knew that Marcus was well aware that him rubbing his fingers through her thick black hair was one surefire way to turn her on. "That's beside the point," Marcus said. "You not deletin' them." He lay his head back onto the top of the couch. "Stop playin' with a nigga. You know you wanna see him."

Kayla, looking up into her man's eyes, smiled. Slowly, she pulled back the waist of Marcus' sweatpants back. Before long, he had lifted up a little so she could pull his pants far enough down to where his manhood popped out. The head thumped against his stomach.

"Suck that shit," Marcus said, rubbing the top of Kayla head.

Within seconds, the room was consumed with slurping noises. Kayla went down on Marcus as he groaned, loving how silky her mouth felt. With just a little encouragement from his hand, Kayla was soon enough able to take about half of his length. Without even thinking, Marcus pulled her head up and kissed her. "I love you," he said.

Kayla smiled, wiping her mouth. "I love you too."

Kayla went back to pleasuring Marcus for a few more minutes before Marcus was lifting up.

"What you doin'?" she asked, confused by what was going on.

Grabbing the waist of his sweatpants with one hand, Marcus used his other hand to pull Kayla away from the couch. "Come on," he told her in a very commanding voice. "I'm about to wear that pussy out."

Without being told any further, Kayla rose up off of the couch and Marcus followed her back to his bedroom. Marcus' bedroom was an alright size, but the way he had it laid out made it look all the more bigger. His dresser and the table that his television sat up on were not bulky. In the corners were little piles of clutter, but they were easy to overlook. Quickly, Marcus pulled Kayla's tense body onto his queen size bed and started kissing her.

"I'm bout to beat that pussy up," he whispered between kisses.

Kayla giggled. "Oh, yeah?" she said, grabbing his rock hard dick.

Marcus smiled, nodding. "Hmm, hmm," he said in response.

Just then, Marcus leaned forward with Kayla bent over his own body, and pulled her pants then panties down to her knees. "Take that shit off," he told her.

Without having to be told twice, Kayla leaned up and removed her pants and panties. Soon enough, they were lying in a little pile on the floor. Marcus stood up, his feet creaking against the hardwood beneath where the two of them stood. In one quick swoop, he pulled his own sweatpants down. Now, he stood naked while embracing Kayla. The rising sun, which was bright because of the untouched white snow outside, shined through the blinds. Slits of light shined across the room, only accentuating the difference in skin tones between the chocolate that was Marcus' skin and the caramel that was Kayla's. With the palm of his hand fully stretch out, while the two of them kissed, Marcus slapped Kayla's phat ass. He grabbed a handful of one cheek and played with it, jiggling it back and forth in his hand and smiling.

"You know you got a phat ass, right?" he said when they broke off from kissing.

Kayla smiled and halfway giggled, knowing that ever since the two of them had met that Marcus had practically worshiped her body. He had always made her feel so good about it, even on days or nights where she was unsure of herself.

"I know how I'mma fuck you," Marcus said.

Before Kayla could even ask what was going on, Marcus was helping her up onto the bed. Softly, he pressed the palm of one of his hands into her neck as he pushed her head into the stack of pillowed pushed up against the bed's headboard. Kayla knew better than to resist. She could tell by the way that Marcus was moving oh so gently, and the way he breathed a steady pace while his dick stayed up and rock hard, throbbing when the head pushed against different areas of her body as he moved, that he woke up really thinking about her.

"A nigga woke up with this shit on his mind," Marcus said as Kayla's body was now in his favorite position – bent over with her ass in the air, her back arched, and her head lying sideways on a pillow. "Damn that pussy look good," he added, reaching underneath her then fingering her.

Kayla moaned. "Damn, nigga," she said. "Now you the one that's playing."

Marcus looked up and over at Kayla's face, shaking his own head as he could see the smile on her face that no matter how hard she tried she could just not wipe away. "I knew you wanted this shit," Marcus said, confidently. "Chill out, chill out. I'm bout to put it on you."

Just then, Marcus jumped up onto the bed and gripped Kayla's hips from the back. Kayla let out a deep grown as she felt Marcus slowly push into her insides. At first, the stretching was a little painful, as it always was. However, as usual, once her insides adjusted, she was practically in heaven.

"Fuck," Kayla said, the world just rolling off of her tongue and into the room. "Damn this dick feel good."

"You know you want some of this dick," Marcus said, between taking deep breaths. He slapped her ass hard. "Don't you?"

Kayla nodded, feeling Marcus as he pushed all the way inside of her – the point where his balls slapped against her body. "Hmm, hmm."

From this point on, Marcus handled his business the way any real nigga would. With a firm grip on Kayla's waist, he long-stroked his manhood into her slowly for several minutes. Soon enough, he could really get into his stroke because Kayla was starting to loosen up. As he sped up, really digging deep into her insides, Marcus's hand slid up the small of Kayla's back then up to her neck. With one hand firmly gripping the back of Kayla's neck while the other held her waist and held her in place, Marcus grinded into her at a steady pace. Kayla moaned as Marcus groaned, telling him how deep he was inside of her. Hearing those words only turned Marcus on more.

About five or six minutes into it, Marcus grabbed both of Kayla's hips and flipped her over. Now, he deep stroked into her missionary style. Their faces pressed against the others.

"Damn, this pussy," Marcus said, softly then kissed Kayla. "A nigga woke up wantin' some of this shit."

"It's yours," Kayla told him. "It's yours."

Putting his best stroke forward and making sure that he did not pull too far back and slip out, Marcus spent the next several minutes giving Kayla those killer deep strokes like you would see in a porn video. Kayla squirmed and squealed as she came a couple of times, loving how rock hard Marcus' manhood felt as it slid in and out of her. The little bit of pain she felt when he went into her balls deep soon enough became pleasure as he was constantly hitting her spot. Her legs tingled in a way that only he could make her feel.

"Fuck, this pussy," Marcus groaned. "I'm bout to bust," he announced. "You on your pill, right?"

"Yeah, nigga," Kayla answered, her eyes closed as Marcus went to licking her nipples.

"Aight then," Marcus said. "Hold on."

On that note, Marcus went full throttle. Soon enough, the back of the headboard was bumping against the wall with the constant rhythm of his deep stroke. At that moment, he could give two shits if the neighbors could hear his banging or Kayla's squealing. With what he was packing, that was just what came with the territory.

"Fuck, I'm bout to nut," Marcus announced. Now, going as fast as he could, his pelvis slammed into Kayla's over and over again before his body stiffened. Before either of them knew it, Marcus' sweaty, toned chocolate body was jolting as he came deep inside of her. Without even thinking, Kayla gripped Marcus' muscular back and smiled.

"Damn, that felt good," Kayla said.

Marcus, trying to catch his breath, decided against saying anything. Instead, he pulled his head up from breathing deeply into the pillows and kissed Kayla passionately. "I love you girl," Marcus said. "I love you. I really do."

There, on this cold Indiana morning, Marcus lay on top of Kayla's body until his manhood softened and slid from the depths of her insides. Marcus slid his hand to the under part of Kayla's thighs and slapped them. "Damn that pussy," he said. "You feel better now?"

Kayla, feeling what can only be described as bliss, pulled the sheets up over her quivering body as Marcus lay down next to her and held her body against his body. "Hmm, hmm," she said.

The two talked back and forth to one another about nothing in particular. Within fifteen to twenty minutes, Kayla was falling back to sleep. There, in the morning light in his bedroom, Marcus looked up at the ceiling. He could not help but to think about the one thing he needed to talk to Kayla about. He just did not know how he was going to bring it up.

Chapter 2

Next thing that either Marcus or Kayla knew, the two of them had fallen asleep in Marcus' bed. Kayla felt so comfortable, at first in his arms then simply with her body pressed against his body. With the sound of trucks and traffic slushing down Shadeland Avenue not too far away, the two of them happened to wake up at the same time. Marcus smiled at his woman, knowing that he had decided before he went to sleep that he was going to have to go ahead and bring up what had been sitting at the back of his mind.

"Hey," Kayla said, looking into Marcus' face. She knew deep down that she felt so much better than she did when she had first gotten over to Marcus' place. "How you feelin?"

"Shit," Marcus said, turning over and looking at his patio door. "I'm good."

"Fuck," Kayla said. "How long was we sleep for?" Her body was stiff, telling her that she had been sleep for some time.

Marcus shrugged and smiled. "Fuck if I know," he responded. "It don't matter no way."

Just as Marcus was sliding his hand over to grab Kayla's waist, he could hear the sound of a vehicle breaking just outside of his apartment. Like a dog, Marcus picked up on it. Without even thinking, his head snapped back toward his patio door. If there was one thing he hated about his apartment it would have to be how the patio door in his bedroom was on the ground level. Every so often, kids playing with a ball out in the parking lot would accidentally hit his window.

"What?" Kayla asked, totally picking up on how alert Marcus suddenly had become. "What's wrong?"

Kayla's voice was slowly sliding to the background for Marcus. Instead, he was too focused on whatever breaking vehicle was outside of his apartment. Quickly, Marcus slid out of bed. Kayla looked at the back of his tall, dark lean body as Marcus stepped over to the long white blinds that covered the patio door. Ever so slightly, Marcus approached the blinds and parted two to look out.

"Marcus?" Kayla said, sounding more forceful this time. "What the fuck is up?"

Without even thinking, Marcus held his hand back toward Kayla. "Wait a second," he said as he looked out into the parking lot. Upon looking side to side, he saw the stopped vehicle was for his neighbors upstairs. Within seconds, he could hear a door upstairs shut then footsteps coming down the hallway steps. Instantly, his heart stopped beating so fast. He turned around.

"Naw," Marcus said, trying to quickly come up with something that would make sense to Kayla without giving too much away at the same time. His head shook as he spoke. "I thought it might be this nigga who was try'na meet up and get a QP. Somethin' happen to dude's phone so he just show up for now until he get himself another phone. I just thought it might be him, but it ain't shit."

Kayla nodded. "Hmm, hmm," she said, not really believing what she was being told. "You jumped up like you was about to have to lock this place down."

Marcus climbed back into the bed, scooting closer to Kayla. He shook his head. "Baby," he said, sounding ever so sweet. "You ain't gotta worry 'bout no shit popping off over here. Just chill out."

"Oh, aight," Kayla said. "I was about to say."

Just then, Kayla winced at the feeling of Marcus slapping her hip. "You wasn't bout to say shit," Marcus said to her, smiling.

"Nigga, whatever," Kayla said. "You betta stop."

Marcus looked into Kayla's face. He generally did not consider himself to be the kind of dude who got emotional. However, in the last so many days he had been thinking about how much he connected with Kayla compared to other chicks he had dated in some way or another before he met her. When Kayla started talking, all he could do was focus on how pretty she was. On top of all that, Kayla was so well spoken and she had a body that made his day better any and every time he laid eyes on her. While he kept his alert up for a car coming to a stop outside of his place, Marcus decided that there was probably no better time than the present to bring it up.

"What do you think about Atlanta?" Marcus came out and asked.

Kayla, taken aback by such a strange and off topic question, clearly looked confused. "What you mean what do I think about Atlanta?" she asked then shrugged. "I mean," she said, hesitantly. "It's cool. I been down there a couple times when I was a teenager with my mama and auntie and shit, but I ain't thought that much more about it all like that. Why you ask what I think about Atlanta?"

"Cause," Marcus answered, shrugging. "I been just thinking."

"Thinking what?" Kayla asked, always enjoying when she and Marcus talked about serious things.

"Shit," Marcus said, very laid back. "Just thinking about maybe moving down to Atlanta or something."

Kayla's eyes bugged out of her face and she leaned up to be more focused on what she was hearing. "Oh, really?" Kayla asked, confused. "Where did all of this come from all of the sudden, Marcus? What got you wanting to move down south to Atlanta and shit? I mean..."

"I just been thinking about it for a while," Marcus said, knowing that he was lying. "I mean, don't you get tired of living in Indianapolis. Sometimes I be just thinking and shit and for the last couple months I really been thinking about what if we move down to Atlanta?"

"We?" Kayla asked. "I mean," she said, trying to think. "Why are you just now bringing this up if you been thinking about it for a couple of months, Marcus?"

Marcus could sense Kayla getting a little worked up over the topic. And in all honesty, it was to be expected.

"I mean, I been thinking about it but not like that," Marcus said. "What you was talkin' bout when you came over in the morning when you dropped your brother and sister off at school just got me to thinking about it a little more." He shrugged. "I mean, it could be like a fresh start and shit for us.

Plus you know Atlanta got more of the scene and shit like what we like that Indianapolis would have."

"Yeah," Kayla said, nodding. "I know, but still...I don't know if I could move away right now. I mean, we don't even live together."

"Kayla," Marcus said. "Baby, you know that if we was to be moving out of town together, we definitely gon' be stayin' together and shit."

"I know, I know," Kayla said. "But we ain't never even been to Atlanta or no shit like that."

"So?" Marcus said, shrugging and smiling as he looked into Kayla's eyes. "Next weekend."

"Next weekend what?" Kayla asked.

"Next weekend we can hop in the car and head down there," Marcus said. "Not unless you gon' be busy."

At that moment, Kayla could feel a little bit of embarrassment coming over her. She hated that she was at a point in her life where she was finally an adult. However, with what was going on with her mother and how she was basically just giving up on herself, Kayla knew what her moving away really meant. Her brother and sister would be left to basically fend for themselves with Mama. And that would definitely be something that would eat away at her soul.

"I mean," Kayla said, trying to find her thoughts. "We can take a trip down there, but I gotta think about movin' down there."

"What you gotta think about?" Marcus asked.

"I mean, this shit is just all of the sudden, Marcus," Kayla said. "You can't just drop something like this on me one night, all of the sudden, and expect me to make a decision. Atlanta is what? Like eight hours away or something."

"So?" Marcus said.

"So?" Kayla said, rhetorically. "I mean...I gotta think about doing some stuff like that. What is the real reason you wanna move down south to Atlanta?"

"What you mean what is the real reason I wanna move down to Atlanta?" Marcus asked. "What's wrong with a change of scenery? Something different. Just some place new. Don't you get tired of livin' in Indianapolis?"

Kayla hesitated. She supposed that she did get tired of living in Indianapolis from time to time. However, Indianapolis was all that she had ever known. She had been on a couple of trips to other places with her family and stuff, but she never stayed anywhere longer than a few days. In fact, Kayla did not even have that many members in her family who lived outside of the Midwest – outside of places like Indianapolis, Chicago, or Detroit.

"I mean, yeah," Kayla answered. "But I ain't really think about moving away or nothing, and especially not all the way down to Atlanta."

"What is keeping you here?" Marcus asked. It was painfully obvious to his woman that there was something in Indianapolis that was pulling her to not even ever think about moving away. "Tell me, Kayla. What you got here?"

Kayla looked away from Marcus, telling him that she did not really want to answer that question. After a few seconds of thought, Kayla decided she had nothing to lose by keeping it real and letting Marcus know how she was really feeling.

"My brother and sister," Kayla answered. "You know I been tellin' you about what's goin' on with my mama and shit. And I swear Marcus, she is just getting worse."

"Yeah, I can see that," Marcus said. "She's the one bein' a young chick again while you usin' your young years to stay at home at night and shit and do whatever the fuck she want you to be doin' so she ain't got to do it her damn self."

Kayla squinted. "You not gettin' angry over that shit, are you?" she asked Marcus.

Marcus shook his head and smiled. "Naw, baby," he answered, trying to sound as nice as possible. "I ain't getting angry over what you doin'. Actually, the shit I don't like is what it is doin' to you, Kayla."

Kayla grinned. "I know, I know," she said. "I mean, I know it's affecting us and shit. I can't even come over the same way I used to. But if I move away, what does that mean for Latrell and Linell?"

Marcus cringed ever so silently. He had a feeling down in his soul that Kayla's brother and sister were the real reason behind her not being all that keen on moving away.

"So, what?" Marcus said, knowing that he had to watch what he said. "You gon' stay around here until they grow up and shit and not live your life?"

"I mean," Kayla said, trying to find the words in her confusion. "Wait a second. Somethin' don't feel right, Marcus. Keep it real and shit with me. Why you really thinkin' 'bout moving down to Atlanta? Why you mentioning it just now?"

"Cause," Marcus said. "I'm bored here and I just been thinkin' bout it more and more and I finally decided to bring it up, if that's okay."

"So, if I don't go, you gon' move away and leave me here?" Kayla asked. "Is that what you thinkin' bout doin?"

Marcus shook his head. "Hell naw," he answered. Just then, Marcus leaned in and kissed Kayla softly. It was obvious to him that what they were talking about made her tense, maybe even a little scared. "What kinda question is that?" he asked. "You know no matter what, I love you and I ain't gon' leave you here like that. Calm down, okay? I was just asking you and lettin' you know what I be thinkin' about and shit. Remember? You told me that you wanted me to start talking more about what be on my mind rather than just keeping the shit inside like I used to do."

Kayla smiled a little. "Yeah," she said. "I mean, I'm not opposed to it. I don't wanna say no and be totally closed to the idea. Maybe…maybe we can take a trip down there and see and stuff. I mean, like I said, I ain't even been there in like years…like since I was a teenager or in middle school. I don't even remember the city all that much like that to be up and deciding to move down there."

"Bet," Marcus said. "Look here. Next weekend, no matter how much snow there is or if there's no snow at all, we gon head down to the A-T-L and check it out. Even if you not feelin' it for movin' there and shit, we can just go there and check it out. I'm ready to get out of Nap so bad. I'm so bored with this shit… I mean damn."

"Yeah," Kayla said. "That would be cool. We prolly just need to get away."

At that moment, Marcus climbed out of bed again. He grabbed his cell phone off of the little table next to his bed and scrolled through his text messages. "Shit, it's like one o'clock."

"Damn, already?" Kayla asked.

"Yeah," Marcus said. "You gotta go pick up your brother and sister?"

"Naw," Kayla answered. "But I'mma be home when they get home from school and shit. You know how my mama is."

"Prolly be passed out and shit when you get there," Marcus said.

"Exactly," Kayla said, rolling her eyes. "That's why I just don't know about moving away cause my brother and sister really would have nobody at that point."

"I feel you, I feel you," Marcus said, setting his iPhone back down onto the little table. He then walked back over to his patio door and peered through the blinds.

Something was definitely up in Kayla's eyes. More and more, she was wanting to know what it was. Something just did not seem right to her. It almost seemed as if Marcus was trying to hide something. Why was he looking out of his blinds so much? He didn't do this all the time, and Kayla knew that for a fact. There she lay, spread out across the bed while looking at the back of Marcus' naked body as he stood at his patio door, parting two blinds ever so slightly and looking side to side.

Kayla took this as her opportunity to slide out of the bed.

"I gotta pee," Kayla said, walking out of the room and into the little hallway that connected Marcus' bedroom to the living room and kitchenette. Within seconds, she was sitting on the toilet with the bathroom door pushed closed and her face in the palms of her hands. While she was not crying – not the least bit – she was indeed thinking about how different her life would be if Marcus did decide to go on and do him and move to Atlanta. Marcus was really the first long-term dude that she had ever had who she felt she could really trust. The odds of her finding that again were next to none in Kayla's eyes. Still, however, she wondered why he was suddenly talking about moving away. Ever since they woke up and he started to look out of the patio door when there was that braking sound, something just did not sit well with Kayla about it all. Maybe it was her woman's intuition kicking in, or just the fact that she was a strong, intelligent woman. However, Kayla just could not help but to think that Marcus was hiding something. In so many ways, it looked like he was looking out of his window because he was watching for someone.

Once Kayla had finally relaxed enough to where she started to pee, she knew what she had to do. She and Marcus were so close that the only way she could not see how he would ever feel like he would have to keep anything from her. When she finished peeing, she stood up, flushed and then started washing her hands.

"Oh shit," Marcus said, from the other room. The tone in his voice made it very clear that he was alarmed.

No sooner than Kayla could open her mouth to yell to him, asking what he had said that for, gun shots rang out – gun shots that were clearly coming at Marcus' apartment building or very close. Without even thinking, screams and shrills slipped out of Kayla's mouth. First, out of reflex, her body jerked back to where her back was flush against the bathroom door. As the gunshots continued, with pinging noises and noises that sounded as if the bullets were colliding with the walls of the apartment building, Kayla dropped to the floor. Never in her life had she been this close to gunshots. It was so scary and surreal at the same time. For the sake of her own life, Kayla ducked as low as she possibly could to the bathroom floor. The sound of the running bathroom sink practically seemed like the background noise that is a clock ticking as what must have been a dozen bullets sprayed into the building, each with a boom that made Kayla's heart practically jump. Still, she screamed as she wished that she could get even lower than the floor.

A window shattered.

Another window shattered.

Within seconds, the bullets stopped. A car door slammed on the back of what sounded like a couple of guys yelling curse words back and forth to one another. Within seconds, Kayla could hear screeching brakes. Whatever vehicle it was had pulled off, zooming away.

Breathing heavily, with her body practically balled up into a corner next to the toilet and cattycorner to the bathtub, Kayla finally opened her eyes. She looked around the bathroom, seeing that there were no holes in the wall. Slowly but confidently, Kayla reached up and turned the running bathroom sink water off.

"Oh my God," she said, not being able to take what now seemed like a deafening silence. "What the fuck happened? What the fuck happened?" Just then, she thought about Marcus. He was not knocking at the bathroom door, nor was he talking from the bedroom. Her eyes bugged out of her face again as she looked at the wall that separated the bathroom from Marcus' bedroom. "Marcus!" she yelled. "Marcus!"

There was no response. Rather, upon trying to calm down a little, Kayla could hear what sounded like Marcus groaning – a sound that definitely let her know that he was in some sort of pain. Kayla jumped up and pulled the bathroom door open. Quickly, she looked both ways, for no particular reason, before hurrying back into Marcus' bedroom. As soon as she stepped across the threshold, her hand instantly covered her face. Within the flash of a second, a tear was strolling down her cheek and her noise was getting stopped up. Standing there, in the doorway of Marcus' bedroom, Kayla could see his long, dark muscular legs sprawled across the floor on the other side of the bed, in the space between the patio door and his bed. Kayla rushed around the front of the bed and leaned down to Marcus.

"Marcus!" she yelled, kneeling over his body. "Marcus, baby? Marcus? Marcus, Marcus, Marcus."

Marcus' eyes barely fluttered open. Once Kayla turned his body over some and looked into his face, she could see that he had been hit in his shoulder. Blood was coming out of him so fast that she just did not know what to do. Tears rolled down her cheeks uncontrollably while her heart beat fast and her emotions ran high on alert. Even her own breathing seemed loud and thunderous.

"Marcus, what is going on?" Kayla asked, frantically. "What is going on?"

Marcus smiled a half-smile and looked into his woman's eyes. "Kayla," he said, softly then coughed a little. "A couple niggas in this black car pulled up…"

Marcus' eyes were starting to close, showing Kayla that he was losing consciousness.

"Marcus, baby," Kayla said, trying to keep him awake. "Marcus, Marcus."

"Yeah," Marcus responded. "Two niggas rolled up and just started firing."

Kayla decided at that moment that she had to take action. Immediately, she grabbed his phone and called the police. After giving them a quick rundown of what had happened, or what she had heard happen since she was in the bathroom, she stayed on the line as the dispatcher instructed. Following the dispatcher's instructions, Kayla quickly grabbed a towel from the bathroom and covered where Marcus had been hit. If nothing else, she wanted to stop the bleeding.

"I called the police, Marcus," Kayla let him know. "I called the police. Just hang on, okay. Just hang on."

"You…" Marcus said, obviously struggling to stay conscious let alone put together coherent sentences. "You ain't get hit, did you?"

Kayla shook her head. "No," she answered. "No I didn't. I was in the bathroom when it happened and I got down to the floor real quick when I started hearing them shooting. Marcus, something is just not right. What is going on?"

"I…" Marcus started to explain. "I told you."

"Naw, I mean what is really going on," Kayla said. "Who are these dudes that rolled up and just started shooting at your place? Who is they, Marcus?"

Marcus was obviously, and thoughtlessly, trying to shrug his shoulder. He winced as a sharp pain rippled through his body.

"Don't move, Marcus," Kayla told him. "Don't try to move. Just tell me who they were."

"I…" Marcus said. "I just saw them roll up and one dude…one dude hopped out and shit and just started shooting."

"And you didn't recognize any of their faces so I can tell the police when they get here?" Kayla asked.

Marcus shook his head and remained silent, his blinks now getting longer and longer as the seconds and the minutes passed with Kayla kneeling over his bloody body.

"Marcus?" Kayla asked.

"Naw, baby," Marcus answered, in a way that was clearly letting her know that he just did not want to say. "I ain't know them niggas."

Kayla nodded. She then realized that the two of them did not even have any clothes on since taking their nap together. She knew she would just have a few more minutes before the police and ambulance came rolling into the parking lot of the apartment complex. With that in mind, she quickly slid into what she had worn over to his place. Frantically, never feeling so scared that her dude might die right there on the floor in front of her, Kayla pulled his dresser drawer open. She dug through until she found a pair of his sweatpants then went back over to him and slid them up his legs.

Marcus chuckled.

Kayla smiled, looking into his eyes. "Nigga," she said. "What the fuck could you possibly be laughing at a time like this? You know you shot in the shoulder, right?"

Marcus nodded again, again letting out a little chuckle. "You," he said. "Thanks for covering my shit up before the police get here."

"Of course," Kayla said.

Within seconds, sirens blared into the air. While they were indeed still at a distance, they sounded like an ambulance and God only knows how many police cars.

"The police is almost here, Marcus, okay?" Kayla said, pushing the towel into his wound. "They almost here, they almost here."

"Good…" Marcus said, his voice clearly getting weaker. "Good. Fuck, it's cold."

Kayla's heart started to beat faster and harder as the tears were just streaming down her face, uncontrollably left and right. She was never really into learning stuff in the medical field but she knew that if a gunshot victim was talking about they were feeling cold, that was not a good sign.

Seconds later, tires screeched against the snow out in the parking lot.

"They here, they here," Kayla said, jumping up. Quickly, she ran into the living room and opened the door so there would be no confusion about which apartment. She waived her arms at the EMT crew, then the police car that swooped in behind their ambulance. Moments later, Marcus' usually very calm apartment was virtually like a crime scene Kayla had seen on television and in movies. It was all just too much, watching a bunch of people in uniforms rush in and head back to the bedroom. While she watched them carry Marcus outside, covering his body with a very thick kind of blanket before going out into the cold winter wind, Kayla found herself getting emotional. At this point, Marcus was not responding in the same way he had minutes earlier. His eyes were closed as he was rolled by her, only opening ever so slightly as he disappeared into the back of the ambulance. Now, this left Kayla to deal with the police and their questions – to do the thing she hated the most.

***

Kayla knew what she had to do to deal with the police. Quickly, she grabbed Marcus' phone from the bedroom and put it into her pocket. After answering the police's questions, giving them as much detail as she could about what she had heard from the bathroom, she really did not feel like she was all the much of a help. Marcus had told her that he did not know who the dudes shooting into his apartment were. However, Kayla was convinced that he probably did and was trying to keep her safe by just not telling her. Nonetheless, she made it a point to cooperate with the police. However, she did feel herself tensing up a little when the police officer asked where Marcus worked. Remembering how Marcus had things laid out, and how he had always told her, Kayla told the police that he worked at his uncle's store over on Clifton. With saying that, she could tell the police really did not believe that answer. Any store over on Clifton would not pay Marcus enough to have an apartment like he had. However, that was the only answer Kayla had and she was going to stick with it.

Once Kayla was done giving her statement to the police, she was feeling a little agitated. She hated how they would send multiple uniforms to ask her the same questions. She made sure to give them all the same answers because she knew that the system was just looking for any reason to look a nigga up, even if he was clearly the victim of the shooting. As she stepped outside with the officers, the ambulance was pulling off. At that moment, an officer came walking up with good news: it looked like Marcus was going to make it. He had lost a lot of blood, but because there was a quick response and he did not get hit in any major organs, he would more than likely be okay.

"Thank God," Kayla said, feeling her emotions coming down a little bit.

Kayla asked what hospital Marcus was being taken to and without a second thought, she hopped into her car and headed toward the highway. Every block seemed twice as far; each stoplight seemed to be red and take twice as long to turn green. In so many ways, she felt frustrated and helpless. As soon as Kayla got onto Interstate 70 and headed toward downtown, she pulled Marcus' cell phone out of her pocket. Careful to watch as she was driving down the highway, she scrolled through his contacts, asking herself who she would call first. She knew that Marcus was close to his daddy, but his mother would probably want to know first. With that thought, Kayla called his mother, Lorna. It was a quick conversation to say the least. She was at work but told Kayla that she would meet her at Methodist, the hospital where Marcus was taken to be treated, which was downtown on 16th Street.

Once Kayla hung up with Lorna, she knew that she had to call Marcus' boys. Ever since Kayla had been talking to Marcus, he and his friends Brandon and Juan had practically been as thick as thieves. If there was any sort of social function going on in the hood, Kayla could bet that one of those two niggas would be there. In many ways, she was almost envious of that because she wished that she had as many friends who really cared for her like Marcus did. However, at the same time, she knew that she was just not as social as Marcus.

Kayla drove as she scrolled through Marcus' contacts until she came across Brandon. She called.

"Wassup nigga?" Brandon answered, clearly assuming that it would be Marcus calling.

"Brandon?" Kayla said. "This Kayla."

Immediately, Brandon was alarmed. "Oh," he said, sounding a little confused as to why his boy Marcus' girl would be calling him from his phone. "Wassup, Kayla?"

"It's Marcus," Kayla said, feeling herself start to tear up again as the sight of Marcus' bloody body popped into her mind again. She kept it together, though.

Immediately, Brandon turned down whatever music was playing in the background. "Marcus?" he asked. "What, Kayla? What happened to my nigga?"

Kayla sniffled. "He on his way to Methodist," she answered. "He got shot, Brandon. He got shot."

"Shot?" Brandon asked. "When? Where?"

"We was at his place chillin'," Kayla explained. "I got up to go to the bathroom and next thing I know, there are gun shots coming into the apartment. Like a dozen or something, I don't know. I just got down on the floor as low as I could. When I came out, that's when I found him."

"Found him?" Brandon asked, clearly concerned about his boy.

"Yeah, Brandon," Kayla said. "I found him on the floor in his bedroom. He got hit by one of the bullets that came through his patio door."

"Damn," Brandon said. "You serious?"

"Yeah," Kayla said. "In the shoulder. Brandon, there was….there was…there so much blood." At the end of her sentence, Kayla could not help her emotions. She was now on the verge of breaking fully into tears from it just being so much to deal with and think about.

"Fuck," Brandon said. "And you headed to the hospital now?"

"Yeah," Kayla said, wiping her face. "I'm headed downtown right now."

"Aight then," Brandon said. "Let me hit Juan up and we gon' see you down there."

"Okay," Kayla said.

Just as Kayla was about to hang up, she heard Brandon say her name.

"What?" Kayla asked.

"Where you tell the police that Marcus work?" Brandon asked.

"At his uncle store," Kayla said. "Or at least, that's what he told me to tell anybody if they ever asked."

"Good deal," Brandon said. "I'mma hit Roy up and tell him what happened. I know that he is gonna wanna know this shit. This shit is fucked up. Just foul. I hope he gon' be alright, man. I hope my boy gon' be alright."

"They told me that he would be," Kayla let Brandon know. "When I was coming outside with the police, there was a officer who walked up and told me that he had lost a lot of blood, but since he was not hit in a important organ, he would more than likely be okay."

"Bet," Brandon said. "I'mma see you down at the hospital, Kayla. Let me hit up Roy and let him know his nephew got hit. This shit fucked up. I'm sure he gon' wanna know about this."

"I mean, who would do some shit like this?" Kayla asked. "In fuckin' broad daylight, just roll up and start shootin' and shit."

"I don't know," Brandon said, in a way that was not totally convincing to Kayla. "Let me call that nigga Roy and I'll see you down at Methodist."

Before Kayla could say anything else, the phone disconnected. Brandon had hung up. For the rest of her twenty minute or so ride into downtown, Kayla had a terrible feeling in her stomach. She felt like she was being kept out of the loop on something, and she really wanted to know what it could be.

Chapter 3

The hospital was the usual sad, funny smelling place. By the time Kayla got there, parked her car, found out what room Marcus was in, and had gotten up there, his mother Lorna was already there. Without even thinking, Kayla and Lorna hugged. In all reality, Kayla had always been rather close to Marcus' mother. At just sixteen years older than Kayla, Kayla always saw Lorna as a bigger sister rather than a motherly kind of woman. She was so pretty and had stayed in shape even after having three kids. Dressed in tight blue jeans and a cute sweater with her hair in a stylish pixie cut, Lorna broke away from her embrace with Kayla and wiped the tears away from her eyes.

"What they say, Miss Lorna?" Kayla asked, looking passed her and into Marcus' hospital room.

Lorna held her head up. "The doctor said that he lost a lot of blood and stuff," Lorna explained. "But he gon' be alright. They operating on him now and asked that I leave the room so that they could have some space and stuff, so I came out here."

"Oh, okay," Kayla said.

"Kayla, tell me what happen," Lorna said. "Please, what the fuck happened?"

Kayla took a deep breath before explaining it all to Lorna. She did not know if Marcus' mother knew what kind of life he was involved in, but she would not be surprised if she did. In fact, even though Lorna was rather polished as she had gotten older, Kayla could tell that she used to be about that life when she was younger. Every so often, she would say something that would let Kayla know that if somebody were to mess with her, they would be messing with the wrong person.

With the explanation now on her mind, Lorna looked back toward the hospital room. "So, you was in the bathroom and somebody just started shooting?" Lorna asked.

Kayla nodded. "I swear," she said. "It was so scary. I didn't know what was happening. I was so scared to come out of the bathroom when the gunshots finally did stop. I'm so sorry. It was just so scary."

"I know, I know," Lorna said. "It's gon' be okay, okay? It's gon' be okay."

Lorna hugged Kayla again, then the two of them sat down in a couple of chairs in a waiting area. Within minutes, the elevator doors opened. Brandon and Juan, both dressed in black hoodies with black jeans sagging and swishing at mid-thigh level, stepped off. Kayla quickly noticed how Lorna rolled her eyes.

"These niggas," Lorna mumbled then shook her head.

"What about'em?" Kayla asked, wanting to know why Lorna's reaction to Marcus' boys was like that.

Lorna just shook her head, letting Kayla know that she would fill her in later.

Brandon and Juan came walking up. Brandon, who was tall and light-skin with tattoos on his neck, practically towered over Juan. Juan was short and kind of pudgy with gold permanents in his mouth. They spoke, being nice.

"What the doctor's say?" Brandon asked.

Kayla and Lorna filled the two of them in not only on what the doctors had said about Marcus' condition, but also on what Kayla had heard and saw happened. Brandon and Juan looked at each other and shook their heads. Once again, Kayla felt like something was just not right. When Kayla glanced over at Lorna, she could see that her eyes were cold as they looked at Brandon and Juan. This made her want to know even more what the tension was about. It was very obvious that Brandon and Juan were not all that well liked by Lorna. When Brandon and Juan walked away and sat in another cluster of chairs in the waiting area, they talked quietly amongst themselves. All the while they talked, Kayla wished that she could hear what they were saying. Her eyes were locked on their mouths, but she really could not make out much of what they were saying. Lorna broke Kayla's focus by tapping her arms ever so slightly. Quickly, Kayla's head jerked to the side and her eyes met with Lorna's eyes.

"What?" Kayla asked.

"What you know about them two niggas?" Lorna asked, glancing over at Brandon and Juan as she barely opened her mouth.

Kayla shrugged. "I mean..." she started. "Them Marcus's boys, I guess. They always chill together and stuff. I called Brandon when it happened and you shoulda heard how he sounded. He got Juan, I guess, and they came right on down here. Why?"

Lorna rolled her eyes. She looked toward Marcus' hospital room then to Brandon and Juan, who were still talking low amongst themselves. When she looked back into Kayla's eyes, she just shook her head.

"No good," Lorna said. "I told Marcus about hangin' out with them niggas. But, you know how that go. Men don't listen...never do."

"Why you say that?" Kayla asked. "Why you say that he shouldn't hang out with them and stuff?"

Lorna made sure to watch her tone. "Ever since Marcus started hanging out with them two," Lorna said. "I just ain't had a good feeling. There was something about them that really got under my skin, if you know what I mean. And I know you probably won't really be able to understand what it is that I'm talkin' about. But it's like a motherly type thing. When it comes to your child, you can just pick up on stuff in the world that you would have never picked up on before. And something about them two niggas used to bug the shit out of me, back when Marcus first started hanging out with them."

At that moment, Kayla was starting to wonder if Lorna knew what kind of life Marcus had going. At the same time, she knew that it was not her place to say. If she brought it up, that would be one thing. However, Kayla knew that she was not going to be the one to bring it up.

"Why you say that, though?" Kayla asked. "I mean...They always seemed cool to me and stuff."

"I guess they would," Lorna said, rolling her eyes. "You know how niggas be. The real likable ones be the main ones that you just can't trust. Anyway, like I was sayin', when Marcus first started hanging out with them two niggas, I remember specifically telling him to watch his back.

Something about them two just ain't seem right to me. You see the way they over there talking and actin' like they don't even know the victim's girlfriend and mother like that."

Kayla glanced over at them and nodded her head. "Yeah," Kayla said, with it all now making sense. "They ain't even hug you, his mama, or anything."

"Exactly," Lorna said. "But let me tell you what I found out about them two like a year and a half ago. So, anyway, I told Marcus about how I felt about them two and, as usual, he said that they was his boys and they was just there for here and all that ole silly shit. Well, I was chillin' over at friend's house – it was like a house party kind of thing, actually – and the two of them came walking through the front door. I was all the way in the back, so they ain't really see me, or at least it don't seem like they did. Plus, you know how I step out when I go somewhere. I was lookin' so good that niggas up in there probably thought that I was in my twenties or something."

Kayla snickered a little bit, loving how confident Lorna was in her looks and knowing that she looked so good as she aged.

"So, anyway," Lorna said. "They stayed and chilled with everybody for a minute, but they was sittin' in the front room. Once they left, after getting something to eat and not really stayin' long, like nigga's do, everything changed."

"What happened?" Kayla asked.

"I'm gettin' there, I'm gettin' there," Lorna said. "My friend, who was chillin' with me in the kitchen was tellin' me that people don't really like when they come around."

Kayla thought about that and was genuinely surprised to hear it. She had never heard the faintest piece of bad information about Brandon and Juan. Sure, they looked rather suspect, but they surely were not the only niggas in all of Naptown to look like that – nothing new for Kayla. She glanced over at Brandon and Juan then back to Lorna as she went on with explaining.

"So, like I was saying," Lorna continued. "Folks got to talkin' and stuff, you know how people do, and come to find out, them niggas had another buddy who got caught up in some shit."

Kayla's eyes opened wide. "Are you serious?" she asked, wondering why Marcus had never mentioned anything like that. She thought about it for a second and it made sense why he would not, however.

Lorna nodded her head. "Girl, yes," she said. "I heard, and don't you go repeatin' this shit before you get caught up in whatever they was, or are, caught up in, but I heard that they got caught up in some shit to where they used to have some friend who now buried up at Crown Hill."

Kayla shook her head. "Naw, Miss Lorna," she said. "You not serious, is you?"

Lorna nodded. "Girl, yes," she said. "And I'm just telling you cause I remember when I was younger and some of the drama I had, I just wish I had somebody to warn me about some of these men. Somethin' ain't right about them two niggas. I don't trust'em any further than I can throw them, if you know what I mean. People at the party was tellin' me that they used to drive down south, I think to Mississippi or somewhere, I get these big ole bunches of weed and shit and drive back up to Indiana, probably working with some Mexicans or something, I don't know. But whatever they was doin', they used to have a third partner, before they met Marcus, mind you, and whoever that third partner is dead and in the ground."

"You think this was a setup?" Kayla came out and asked.

"Girl, don't say that too loud," Lorna told her, glancing over at Brandon and Juan. "But I don't know if it was a set up or maybe if someone was really after them two niggas and thought that maybe they lived over in Marcus' apartment or something. You just never know, especially nowadays with all of these niggas killin' one another. All I know is that whoever they used to hang with, before Marcus, got killed some years back and now my son is sittin' up in the hospital with a bullet lodged in his shoulder. What would you think? Who is the common denominator?"

Kayla nodded, fully understanding exactly what Lorna was telling her. She then thought about how Marcus had clearly been on the lookout before the bullets started flying.

She was sure that whatever reason he was looking out of the patio blinds for, especially when there was that sound of a car breaking, had something to do with this. However, she also knew that Lorna, as a mother, was probably already stressed and really fearful for her child's life, as any mother would be. With that thought, she decided to keep that part to herself and not say anything right then. She just did not want to go and make thing any worse than they already were.

"Look, I can't say what did or did not happen, Kayla," Lorna said. "But I will tell you this. Girl, you betta watch your fuckin' back when it comes to them two niggas. I don't know how you feel about them, but something about them just rubs me the wrong way. I mean, they just seem like they are up to absolutely no good – no good at all. I just wish Marcus would stop hanging out with them kinda people. I told him, cause this is exactly the kind of shit that happens. I don't like this shit one bit, and I just hope that Marcus is gon' be okay and that this will be a wakeup call for him."

Kayla nodded, fully understanding what Lorna was saying. "I feel you," she said.

Just then, a doctor – white man with dark hair and big glasses, dressed in a long white lab coat – came walking up. He smiled.

"Hello, Miss Miller," the doctor said.

Lorna stood up, being fully attentive to whatever was about to come out of the doctor's mouth. Within seconds, the sounds of swishing pants came up behind them. Brandon and Juan, seeing the doctor, come out of Marcus' hospital room, came walking up to see what was goin' on with their boy. Lorna sensed that they were standing behind her and rolled her eyes, wishing that they were not even there.

"We were able to get the bullet out of his shoulder," the doctor said. "Your son lost a lot of blood and he will probably have to be here for at least a couple of days."

"At least he is gon' make it," Lorna said. "That's good enough for me, doctor. At least my boy is gon' make it."

"Yeah," the doctor said. "But he will probably have to undergo physical therapy of sorts. We are not entirely sure how long and to what extent just yet, but I would imagine that it would be a while before he will have full use of his arm again. Once again, I am not totally sure, however."

Lorna nodded. "Thank you, Doctor," she said. "Thank you for letting me know. Can I go in and talk to him now?"

The doctor shook his head. "He is still out," he answered. "And the nurses are finishing up some things. I suspect that he will be waking up within a couple of hours if you would want to wait, which I am sure that you will."

"Of course," Lorna said.

The doctor walked away, heading over toward a nurses station before heading into a different room. Lorna looked at Kayla. "Baby," she said. "I don't know what you got to do today, but you ain't gotta wait up here all day if you don't want. I told my job what happened and that I wouldn't be coming back in today and they cool with that, so I'mma be up here."

"Right, right," Kayla said, as she was thinking. She then thought to look at the time, on her cell phone. It was getting close to the time that Latrell and Linell would be getting out of school. Part of her felt guilty for even thinking of leaving the hospital while Marcus was lying up after being shot; however, at the same time, she knew that there was so little that she would be able to do. "My little brother and sister gettin' out of school in a little bit," Kayla told Lorna. "I prolly should go make sure that they get in the house okay and stuff and I can come back up here."

"Okay, Kayla," Lorna said. She briefly glanced at Brandon and Juan before sitting back down.

Kayla turned around to head for the elevator. Naturally, Brandon and Juan were in her path. They walked her across the lobby and toward the elevator.

"This some fucked up shit," Juan said, with Brandon nodding his head. "And you said that you ain't see the people who did this shit, Kayla?"

Kayla shook her head, trying to be as nice to Brandon and Juan as she would normally be while also thinking about what Lorna had just said to her minutes earlier, before the doctor came out of Marcus' room. "Naw," she said. "I was in the bathroom when the bullets started flying into the apartment and shit. Glass was breaking and everything. Like I said, when

I came out, I found Marcus on the floor in his bedroom. I went over to him and found that he was hit and then called the police and stuff."

Brandon shook his head. "Don't you worry," he said. "We gon' figure out the niggas that did this shit. This shit ain't coo."

"Why would anyone want to get Marcus?" Kayla came out and asked. "I mean, why would anybody want to do this?"

Kayla noticed how Brandon and Juan looked at one another before looking back at her. Something about how they did that told Kayla that there was something that they were holding back. The two of them then shrugged their shoulders.

"I mean..." Juan said, clearly sounding hesitant and sounding like he was trying to think up something to say. "This shit is just fucked up. Naw, we don't know who would do some shit like this, but we gon' ask around and find out."

Kayla nodded as the elevator door opened, feeling like there just might be some truth to Marcus' mother's suspicions.

"So, what y'all bout to do?" Kayla asked.

Brandon looked at Juan then back to her. "Shit," he said. "I guess we just gon' wait till Marcus wake up and shit."

"Cool," Kayla said. "Well, I gotta go home and check on my brother and sister. I told his mama that I'd be back up here later on. I hope that everything gon' be okay."

Brandon nodded. "I do too, I do too."

"Aight then," Kayla said, still not being able to not look at Brandon and Juan in a different light with what Lorna had told her. "I'll see y'all maybe when I come back up here."

On that note, the elevator doors closed. Kayla tried to be strong, keeping the tears back and trying to think positive thoughts. Even though the doctor had said that Marcus would be okay, she still could not get the image of his body on the floor when she came out of the bathroom. Furthermore, she was really getting concerned now about if and when whoever shot up his apartment would come back and try again once word got around that he had been shot and survived. Kayla knew something was up, as she rode the elevator downstairs to the first floor and zigzagged her way through the hospital and to her car in the hospital parking garage.

When Kayla pulled up out front of her house, she could not help but to cringe when she saw that her mother's car was still parked out front. There were times she would come home and find that she was gone. Today, out of any other day of the year, would have been perfect in Kayla's eyes to be one of those days. At least, she took a deep breath and walked right on inside, hoping and praying to God that her mother did not start any shit with her when she walked through the front door. Today was just not the day. Kayla's emotions were running too high.

Kayla unlocked the door and walked into the quiet living room. After pushing the curtains of the front window to the side a little bit to let a little bit of light into the house, she then noticed her mother. There she lay, on the couch, passed out with her legs spread open. Kayla sighed and grunted, hating how her mother would lay around in such a provocative when she had a perfectly good bedroom upstairs that she could go lay in without someone having to walk through the door and see a 40 plus woman with her legs spread out and no cover over her.

"This shit don't make no damn sense," Kayla said to herself as she walked through the living room and into the dining room. As soon as she was making her way around the dining room table, she heard her mother waking up.

"What was that?" her mother, Rolanda, asked.

Kayla shook her head and rolled her eyes. "Nothin', Mama," she answered and walked into the kitchen. In the kitchen, she opened the refrigerator and got herself something to drink while she leaned against the countertop and reflected on everything. Within a matter of seconds, her mother was making her way across the dining room and into the kitchen. Without even thinking, Kayla shook her head and turned around, now facing the window over the kitchen sink. "This bitch," she mumbled.

"What was that?" Rolanda asked, now standing in the kitchen doorway.

Kayla finished her drink then set the cup down into the sink, shaking her head. "I ain't say nothin," she said.

"I thought I told you when you left this morning to come back with my car when you dropped Latrell and Linell off at school, huh?" Rolanda asked. "What the hell happened with that, Kayla?"

Kayla turned around and faced her mother, deciding that she was just going to keep it real and let her know what happened.

"I went and saw Marcus," Kayla said. "If that is alright with you."

"Ain't no reason to get an attitude or anything, Kayla," Rolanda said. "I was just askin'. And since you ain't got no car of your own, and you live under my roof, maybe you should be getting Marcus to come over here and pick you up. I know he don't live nearby or nothin', but if the nigga really did care for you, I am sure that he would have no problem coming over to the west side and picking you up. What are we from the highway exit? Like less than a mile?"

"Well," Kayla said. "He probably won't be doin' that for a little while now, Mama, so I'm sorry, if that's what you want to hear."

"What the fuck you mean he probably won't be doin' that for a while now?" Rolanda asked. "What happened? He drop you and get himself somethin' better or some shit."

Kayla took a deep breath and closed her eyes for a moment. She swore to herself that if her mother was not her mother, she would have lunged across that room at that very second and let her know what he really thought. And there would have been very few words exchanged at that. Kayla just shook her head. "No, Mama," she said. "So here's what happened. I was over at his place, chilling like we always do."

"You was over there fuckin'," Roland said. "Girl, don't act like I was born yesterday or some shit. I ain't stupid." The two of them squinted at one another. "Okay, go ahead," Roland encouraged. "So, what happened?"

"Like I said," Kayla said. "I was over at his place, chilling, like I said, and…"

Rolanda could sense that Kayla was starting to talk about something that was very personal to her. She lightened up a little bit, wanting to know what all it was.

"And what?" Rolanda asked, sternly.

"Mama," Kayla said, starting to have second thoughts about whether or not she should even tell her mother what all had happened. She decided, though, that sooner or later, she would have to know or she would probably find out. After all, Indianapolis is a big city if you're white, but if you're black, the world becomes such a smaller place. "Somebody shot his apartment up."

Rolanda practically choked on the words that were about to come out of her mouth. "Shot his apartment up?" she asked. "What are you talkin' bout, Kayla?"

"Just what I said, Mama," Kayla said. "I was over there and somebody shot up his apartment. Guns and bullets, you know the kind of thing."

"Girl, watch your mouth," Rolanda said, now coming closer. "Okay, so you was in there, chillin' or whatever, and somebody rolled up and just started shooting at his apartment."

Kayla nodded. "Well," she said. "I had just went to the bathroom. When I was washing my hands, that when it started."

"Like how many gunshots, Kayla?" Rolanda asked.

"Oh, hell, Mama," Kayla said, feeling herself start to tear up. "I don't know. It was a light, I do know that. Like I said, I was in the bathroom and next thing I know, bullets started flying into Marcus' apartment. I could hear glass breaking and stuff. I was so scared."

"I bet," Rolanda said. She then could tell that there was more to the story that her daughter was not telling her. "So, what else, Kayla? I know you wasn't gone this long, I mean it's damn near three o'clock in the afternoon because somebody shot up his apartment."

Kayla was hesitant before going ahead and telling her mother the rest of the story. "Mama," she said. "Marcus is in the hospital. He was in his bedroom when the shots started and…and…and…he got hit."

Rolanda's eyes bulged out of her face as she started to shake her head. "No," she said. "Where was he shot at? I mean, what part of his body?"

Kayla looked down at the floor, thinking about how she had found Marcus on the floor in the space between his bed and his patio door. "He was shot in his shoulder," Kayla said. A tear now rolled down the side of her face. "Mama, there was so much blood and stuff. I swear to God, I thought he was gonna die right then and there...I swear I did."

"Okay, okay," Rolanda said, now trying to sound a little more compassionate than she might normally sound. "So then what?" she asked. "I mean, is he in the hospital or what."

"He at Methodist," Kayla answered, pointing to the south. "That's where I was just coming from when I got here, the hospital. The doctor's operated on him and stuff, pulled the bullet out of his shoulder, and came out and told us that he would be okay, but he probably would not be able to use his arm for a long time and something about how he would probably have to go through some physical therapy to get back full use of it like he had before."

Rolanda shook her head. "Well," she said. "I am sorry to hear that. I know that musta been some scary shit. I been in the club more than a few times when shots started ringing out into the air, so I know how that shit feels when you just don't know what the hell is going on and where it's going on. Wait a minute, though. Who is we?"

"Me and Marcus's mama, Lorna," Kayla answered.

"Hmm," Rolanda said. "I'mma be nice and not say no bad about her right now. You know how I feel about her."

"I know, Mama," Kayla said. "I know."

Lorna and Rolanda had gone to high school together back in the day, but they really had never known each other until after they graduated. The two of them, or so Kayla had heard, were deep into that clubbing life. One thing led to another and after some months, they had found out that they were talking to the same dude. As young women, they got into it badly over this guy – a guy who would wind up moving up north to Milwaukee and leaving them both behind like two bad habits. For whatever reason, Rolanda just could never let that go, even if it had been almost twenty years ago.

"Kayla," Rolanda said, now sounding more stern and forceful than she had been sounding over the last few minutes. "I told you what I thought about Marcus. I mean, I like him and all. He seems like a nice guy and stuff, but I just don't know about him. You was over his place and coulda got shot too. I hope you realize that."

"I know, Mama," Kayla said, feeling a little annoyed that her mother was even going there when her own love life was full of thugs and dudes fresh out of the Marion County lockup downtown. "I know."

"Is he still involved in that shit, Kayla?" Rolanda asked.

Kayla looked away, making it very obvious that she did not want to answer.

"Huh, Kayla?" Rolanda asked.

"I don't know, Mama," Kayla said.

Rolanda nodded, knowing that her daughter was playing dumb with her and lying dead to her face right then and there in that kitchen. "Girl, stop with the bullshit," Rolanda said. "You know damn well if the nigga got a job or if he still out in them streets, making money like he been making money. Don't talk to me like I'm stupid."

"Well, I was thinkin' the same about you," Kayla said, sounding very smart-aleck in her tone. "You ain't got no job. How you makin' your money?"

Rolanda scolded Kayla just with her eyes. "Kayla, I know you done had a scary little day," she said. "But hear me when I say this. You not gon be talkin' to me any ole fuckin' way. Don't worry about how I'm makin' my money. Just know that the bills stay paid around here, because of me. You definitely can't say the same, now can you?"

"Whatever," Kayla said, getting tired of how her mother would always throw certain things up in her face. Deciding that she was tired of talking to her mother, she went ahead and starting getting a little something to eat together for Latrell and Linell.

Within minutes, the front door was swinging open. Latrell and Linell came walking in, bickering with each other about something or another while the door stood open and cold wind came rushing into the house.

"Close that fuckin' door!" Rolanda yelled. "Don't be lettin' all my damn heat out."

"Sorry, Mama," Latrell said.

"Yeah," Linell said. "Sorry, Mama. I told him to shut the door, but he wasn't listening."

"Come on in here and get y'all a little somethin' to eat," Kayla announced, before turning around to see what she had for options to cook up quickly.

Latrell and Linell dropped their backpacks and coats onto the couch in the living room and came rushing through the dining room then into the kitchen. Rolanda watched as the two of them pulled out chairs and sat down on opposite sides of the table.

"Kayla," Rolanda said, trying to sound motherly. "I just want you to think about it all and stuff. Don't be that girl who, you know."

"Yeah, Mama," Kayla said. She could not even take her mother seriously when she talked to her like that anymore. There she stood, looking through the refrigerator to make her brother and sister something to eat while their mother obviously was talking out of the side of her neck with her hangover. It got on Kayla's nerves so bad. She could never stand when her mother just had to do the most. "I know."

Rolanda looked at her daughter, remembering when she herself had the body and the beauty that she saw in her own child at this point in life. It was really something to see. However, it also knocked at the pit of her stomach in a way. It had come and gone so fast. By the time she was Kayla's age, she had already had an abortion, then a baby. Thinking about all of this reminded her how she just needed to go finish laying down.

"Alright," Rolanda said. "I'mma go lay back down." She turned around, zigzagged across the dining room, then went upstairs.

Kayla sighed and rolled her eyes. "Yeah, you do that," she said to herself, though responding to what her mother had said just moments before.

"What we eatin'?" Linell asked.

Kayla glanced at her younger brother and sister at the table before shutting the refrigerator door and looking through the cabinets. "Thank you, Jesus!" she said, upon finding some cans of ravioli. She just needed to feed them a little something until later on – when she hoped to God that her mother would take the time to cook dinner. She usually at least did that, even if the food was really things that only she had a hunger for and nobody else.

"Hold up, y'all," Kayla said. "Hold up."

She dumped the ravioli into a sauce pan and began to heat it up. While she did this, she thought about how just hours before she had found her boyfriend on the floor, shot after the two of them were in his apartment when it got shot up. The last thing she really felt like doing was putting any sort of food together. At the same time, she felt like it was probably a good thing that she wasn't going to break up Latrell's and Linell's normal day.

"Remind me to get the food stamp card from Mama when she ain't so busy being a bitch," Kayla said over her shoulder. "We need to get out and get some food. And I know it ain't gon happen unless I do it so I'mma have to do something about that I'm sure."

"Okay," Linell said. "Kayla?"

"What?"

"Wassup with you?" Linell asked.

"What you mean?" Kayla asked, not liking that her nine year old sister could pick up on how she was feeling, or even that she could tell that she was feeling some sort of way.

"You just seem a little mad today," Linell said.

"Yeah," Latrell added. "You seem like you pissed off about somethin' or somethin'."

"I ain't mad about nothin'," Kayla lied. "Just got a lot of my mind. I'm not gon' be home later on tonight, so I hope Mama cook dinner and whatever. I ain't mad, y'all." She thought about the entire situation and how she was in the thick of it but it still did not seem real. "Don't y'all worry. So, what happened at school today?"

Latrell shared his story, about seeing a fight in the gym during recess. Linell talked about how her gym class tried to convince the gym teacher to take them outside to play in the snow instead of staying in the gym. Kayla nodded, adding her own little two cents here and there while she finished heating up the ravioli, then putting it into bowls and in front of Latrell and Linell. The conversation then turned to how the two of them might go out and play in the snow when they get done eating. To Kayla, this would be perfect. This would give her a little time to herself – time where she could sit up in her room and just think. More than anything, she just wanted to think without having to be doing something else – no cooking, no driving, no talking to the police, no talking to Marcus' mama, no talking to Brandon and Juan.

"When y'all finish eating, make sure to put your bowls in the sink before you go out and play in the snow," Kayla said. "And don't be out there all that long, so y'all don't get sick. I don't need no more problems right now, please. Hurry up so y'all can get out there while there is still a lot of sunlight."

Latrell and Linell both agreed to what their older sister was telling them. They then went on to talking amongst themselves while Kayla dropped the sauce pan into the sink and headed upstairs. As soon as she crossed the threshold into her bedroom, she pushed her door close and practically collapsed on the bed. The image of Marcus's bloody body lying on the floor flashed in her mind. It was almost like a movie to her, except the plot starred her and she had to be her own stunt double. Never, in her entire life, had she been so terrified as she had been at those moments when the bullets began flying into the apartment – the moment where she was just washing her hand. A tear rolled down her cheek. Out of instinct, she grabbed her phone. This would be the usual time that Kayla would be texting Marcus. When she remembered that his phone was in the car, she dropped her phone onto the bed next to her.

Brandon and Juan popped into Kayla's mind. As much as she respected Marcus' mama Lorna and truly did listen to anything that she had to tell her, Kayla still did not think of herself as the kind of woman who would just believe anything that somebody told her…even if that somebody was somebody who always kept it real. If there was one thing she had learned out of life so far, it was that even the realest person can get it so wrong at times. Kayla pushed her head into her pillow and closed her eyes as the thoughts consumed her.

Suddenly, her phone vibrated. She quickly grabbed her phone and saw that it was a text from her girl, Myesha. She took a deep breath and looked back at the ceiling, trying to figure out if she felt like talking to Myesha right now or not. Kayla had been best friends with Myesha basically for as long as either of them could remember. Kayla lived at one end of the block while Myesha lived a couple of houses down from the corner of the block to the north. Some years they went to the same schools, while others they wound up going to separate schools. Regardless, even thru some ups and downs, Kayla had remained friends with Myesha for all of this time. Now, however, things were a little different. Myesha was well into her freshman year at IUPUI, which is right downtown. They still hung out when Myesha wasn't busy, and Kayla really was happy for her friend. She had always said that she was going to get a Master's and she at least got on the road to doing so.

Hesitantly, Kayla decided to go ahead and hit her girl up and tell her what had happened. She thought that maybe it would do her some good to talk about it with someone rather than to sit and drown in her own thoughts about it all. She grabbed her phone and called Myesha.

"Hello?" Myesha answered.

"Girl, what you doin?" Kayla asked. "I saw that you text me so I figured I would just call."

"Girl, you cool," Myesha let her know. "And nothing. Just got home from class. Girl, all of this snow is really getting to be too much for me. I wish it would just go away. I mean, how much are we going to get hit with over and over like this? This is ridiculous."

Kayla chuckled. "Yeah, I know what you mean," she said. "It do seem like winter be lasting for fucking ever, don't it?"

"That's what I'm sayin'," Myesha said. "I was texting you to see what you would be doing later on or something."

This was the moment that Kayla knew she might as well go on into her story. She knew damn well that she was going to be at Marcus' bedside for at least a little while tonight, no matter how much snow there would be out on the streets. Methodist Hospital was too close for her not to be down there. Plus, she wanted to talk to him. At the back of her mind, she was starting to think about how he was probably awake and wondering where she was.

"Kayla?" Myesha asked, totally picking up on the long pause – a pause that just was not typical of her girl Kayla. "You there?"

"Yeah," Kayla said. "Yeah. Girl, let me tell you."

"Tell me what?" Myesha asked, clearly ready to hear whatever story was about to come. "Girl, what? What is it?"

"Today," Kayla said, flatly. She rolled over onto her side, now facing the lit window, with the phone balancing on the side of her face. "Today, today, today."

"Girl, what?" Myesha asked.

Kayla sniffled. In so many ways, it was just too much to think about.

"Somebody shot up Marcus's apartment today," Kayla said.

"Oh my God," Myesha said. "Are you serious? I mean, when? Are you serious? Somebody shot his apartment up? Was he there?"

"I was there too," Kayla told her. "It was earlier today. I forget what time right now cause everything has just been going so fast it seem like."

"You was there too?" Myesha asked, clearly very concerned about her best friend. "And, I know. I know what you mean. I bet it has. But what happened?"

"This morning," Kayla said. "After I dropped Latrell and Linell off at school, you know the normal thing, I drove out to Marcus's. You know, like I was texting you yesterday. I was supposed to see him last night, but since my mama wanted to stay wherever she stayed last night, I wound up staying home and playing mother."

Myesha cringed. "Sorry, girl," she said. "But that's nothing new."

"I know it ain't," Kayla said. "I know. But, anyway, so like I said, I drove out there and we was chilling and stuff. After we woke up, I had noticed how he kept checking out of the window, I mean the blinds that cover his patio door. You know he live on the first floor."

"Yeah, I remember you tellin' me that," Myesha said.

"Yeah," Kayla said. "So, anyway, I saw how he kept looking outside, like he was expecting something or someone. Shit, I don't know. I got up and went to the bathroom. Next you know, I hear Marcus say 'oh shoot.' Then there were gunshots and the sound of bullets hitting and shattering the windows." Kayla took a deep breath, almost reliving the very fear that she had felt in Marcus' bathroom. "Girl, I dropped down to the floor so fast. I mean, I never been that scared in my life."

"I thank God nothing like that has ever happened to me," Myesha said. "But, girl, I am glad you didn't get hit. I mean, you don't sound like you did. I don't hear hospital machines and stuff."

"No, I'm fine," Kayla said. "But that's not all of the story, Myesha. Once all of the bullets stopped, I waited before I went out. I don't know what I was doin'. I guess I was waiting to see if I heard footsteps or something, I don't know. But anyway, once I heard a car take off, I waited for some seconds. I started to call Marcus' name and he wasn't responding."

"Oh no," Myesha said.

"I went out there and found him on the floor, girl," Kayla said. "Myesha, they got him in his shoulder."

"Girl, I am so sorry to hear that," Myesha said. "And I mean that, I really am sorry. Did you get him to a hospital?"

"Yeah," Kayla said. "I called the police and an ambulance came. He in Methodist, downtown, so I'mma be up there again later on tonight. I was up there earlier, with his Mama and Brandon and Juan. The doctor came out and told us that he would be fine. Just that he would have to do some physical therapy to get full function of his arm back again. Myesha, girl, when I found him, I swear I was starting to think that he was gon' die. There was blood everywhere, like you wouldn't believe."

"I can imagine," Myesha said. "So, did he say if he saw who did this? I'm not liking this, girl. You need to be careful. And plus, you know these damn Indianapolis police won't do much of that thing they call investigating if it affects us."

"Yeah," Kayla said. "They came and were nice to me and stuff, but I think they are probably just thinking it's another case of hood nigga violence."

"Marcus still don't have no real front, do he?" Myesha asked.

"Naw," Kayla said. "I mean, what was real funny though is how when me and him was layin in bed and stuff, he asked me about moving to Atlanta."

"What?" Myesha said, surprised. "He asked you about doing what? Moving to Atlanta?"

"Yeah," Kayla said. "All of the sudden, he start talkin' about how he tired of Indianapolis and wanna move to Atlanta. Right before I got up to go to the bathroom, we had just talked about taking a trip down there next weekend or something. I said I'd go, but I don't know if I can leave my brother and sister here like that. Not right now and stuff. Plus, if I'm doin' all that kind of thing, moving away with him and stuff, I think I wanna be married or something."

"Exactly," Myesha said. "That is exactly what I'm saying. You would have to put a ring on it for me to even think about moving that far away. I mean, I know Atlanta is nicer than Indianapolis and stuff, but do you even know people down there? Does he even know people down there?"

"That is exactly what I was thinking too, girl," Kayla said. "I don't even think he know anybody down there. To me, though, it was just funny how he start talking about this out of the blue and I'm like, where the fuck did this even come from? Next thing you know, the apartment is getting shot up."

"I hate to break this to you," Myesha said. "But it sound like he caught up in some shit to me…if you ask me."

The words "he caught up in some shit" practically echoed in Kayla's mind like bad sound inside of a stadium. The very thing that she had kind of been avoiding thinking had now confronted her. It had now come from another person who is totally outside of the situation. The crazy part about all of this for her, however, is that she still hadn't even told Myesha about what Lorna had said to her. That would really just put the cherry on top of this story.

"Girl, that's not all," Kayla said, deciding to go ahead and finish with the story. "There's more."

"There's more?" Myesha asked.

"So, I was sittin' at the hospital, in the little waiting area outside of Marcus room with his mama, right?" Kayla said.

"Right, right," Myesha said.

Just then, Kayla could hear the front door open and close downstairs. She knew that it was Latrell and Linell going outside to play in the snow. Within minutes, she could hear them talking amongst themselves out front. She focused back on her conversation with Myesha.

"And Marcus' boys Brandon and Juan come walking off of the elevator," Kayla said.

"You not cool with them anymore or something?" Myesha asked. "What's wrong with that?"

"I mean," Kayla said. "We cool and stuff, I mean... I don't hang out with them like that or anything. It's not like they be over at Marcus's place at the same time that I be over there. The couple of times they have been, they was leaving as I was getting there so it was just a hi and bye sort of thing. Ain't like we go out for drinks or anything like that."

"I see, I see," Myesha said.

"Yeah, so anyway," Kayla said. "They was there and when they went and sat down in the other part of the waiting are, you know, more over towards the elevator door and stuff, Miss Lorna told me how she really felt about them and what she'd heard about them."

"Huh?" Myesha asked. "What she'd heard about them? Girl, tell me."

Kayla filled Myesha in on everything she could remember that Marcus' mama Lorna had told her at the hospital. And of course, Myesha was just about as surprised as Kayla was earlier when hearing about how Brandon and

Juan had had another friend who wound up getting killed back whenever.

"Girl, I know that's yo man and stuff," Myesha warned, completely cutting the conversation off. "But you really need to watch yourself. Girl, you really need to be careful. You know I'm your girl and I love you like a sister. And I really do mean that. But, to me, it sounds as if that nigga done got caught up in some shit. I mean, it is so obvious. I just wonder what, and how far is whoever willing to go for whatever happened. Think about it. You said he was looking out of the window or patio door or whatever and was looking like he was waiting or looking for somebody. Then he suddenly start talkin' about movin' away. Now you say his mama done heard some bad shit about his friends. You know how some niggas are. They will set somebody up in a minute. Wait a second, though. Is Marcus moving like that? Is he really out there like that to where he'd be gettin' that kind of attention?"

Kayla took in everything that her best friend was saying to her. Another tear slid down her eye while her heart pumped lightly with fear. The very idea that whoever had shot up Marcus' apartment could decide to come back and try again just made her tremble. She then started to think about what Marcus talked about with her about how he was doing with making his money. They spent so much time together where they talked about any and everything – that real friend bond was there – and Kayla hated the fact that she was coming up mostly blank on that particular subject. She knew that these were things she probably would not have if it was not for him.

"I guess he doin' good," Kayla said. "I just wanna know who did this, Myesha. This is some scary shit. Just to think…what if they come back?"

"Don't think that," Myesha said. "Don't think that. Plus, they might have just been doin' it to scare him or something."

"Girl, what the fuck you talkin' bout?" Kayla asked. "To scare him? Are you serious? Scaring somebody is like two, maybe three or even four bullets. Whoever came up in his apartments got him with I don't know how many. It was a lot more than four or five, I do know that."

"Awe," Myesha said. "Well damn, girl, you ain't tell me that. Like I said, though, you really need to watch out and shit with this. I don't like this at all. Maybe you better keep your distance until somebody figure out who this is or something. Where is he gon' stay when he get out of the hospital?"

"Girl, I don't know," Kayla answered. "When I left the hospital, he was still knocked out from surgery, so I still haven't got to talk with him. I guess he would probably go stay with his mama."

"I don't know if he should do that," Myesha said. "I mean, they might be people that he knows so they might know where his mama stay. Of course, I don't know, but I'm just saying. He need to stay somewhere that won't nobody be looking for him. I know that is what I would do."

"Well, I don't know," Kayla said. "I'mma talk to him about all of this when I go up to the hospital later on cause I just got too much I need to know first. This has been one fucked up day for me."

"Yeah, it sound like it," Myesha said. "Well, girl, I was just texting you to see what you was up to. Please, think about what I said. Watch yourself cause these niggas is crazy out here nowadays and some of them will kill any damn body."

"Girl, I know," Kayla said, rubbing her forehead.

"Alright," Myesha said. "Make sure you hit me up later when you leave the hospital or something so I know how you feeling."

"Okay, I will."

They hung up the call. Kayla dropped her phone onto her bed and turned over onto her other side. For the next several minutes, she would try to go to sleep. She would go for long spurts of lying there, with her eyes closed, faced away from the bright light of the window. Nonetheless, it did not work. It was like she was tired, but too shaken to go to sleep. There was just too much going through her mind for it to allow itself some rest.

Eventually, she noticed that she could still hear Latrell and Linell talking out in the front yard. Since she didn't know how cold it was supposed to be getting out there, she went ahead and got herself out of bed. She headed downstairs so that she could tell her brother and sister to come inside. The last thing she really needed right then was two sick kids whose own mother could not be counted on to help them.

When Kayla got downstairs to the front door, she pulled it open and cringed as the cold winter wind slammed into her body. She got Latrell and Linell's attention.

"Come on back inside," she said. "Warm up a little bit."

Without arguing, Latrell and Linell dropped the snow they had been playing with and darted up to the front porch and into the living room. Quickly, almost as soon as Linell's foot was over the doorway's threshold, Kayla pushed the door closed.

"Marcus not here, is he?" Latrell asked.

Upon hearing those words, Kayla quickly snapped around and looked at her younger brother. He was pulling his hat off then sliding out of his big black coat. Kayla wondered why in the world Latrell would ask a question like that. It was almost scary how coincidental such a thing could be.

"Naw, he ain't here," Kayla answered. "Why? Why would you ask that?"

"Cause," Linell said.

"Yeah," Latrell said. "These two guys asked and we told them no, but I wasn't sure and we didn't want to come all the way in and ask you."

Kayla felt her heart start beating so fast that it was practically thumping out of her chest. Quickly, she turned around and looked through the blinds and out toward the front yard and street. Calm is the only way to describe what she saw – no people, no cars that she did not know, and a couple of birds in the sky.

"What two dudes?" she asked. "Who the hell were you two out there talkin' to? What did I tell you about talkin' to people that you don't know?"

"I swear, Kayla," Latrell said. "We didn't talk to them. They just stopped as they was goin' down the street and asked if Marcus was here. I just told him that he wasn't."

Kayla rushed passed Latrell and Linell and into the dining room, not even sure herself where she was going. She turned back around and looked at her brother and sister.

"What they look like?" she asked. "What kind of car they was driving?"

Latrell shrugged. "A couple of black dudes," he answered. "And they was in a black car."

"A black car?" Kayla asked, doing so loudly and with her eyes bugged out on her face.

Linell looked at her older sister than to her twin brother. "Yeah, a black car," she said. "Why? What's wrong, Kayla?"

"Yeah," Latrell said. "What's wrong?"

Kayla thought about how some of the last words she had had with Marcus up to this point were about what the people looked like that pulled up in the parking lot and started to fire at his apartment. She was breathing deeply at this point, and her head was starting to shake while her own body trembled.

"Don't worry about it, y'all," Kayla said to her little brother and sister. "Just chill out. You right, Marcus ain't here. I just wanted to know who it was that would be asking if Marcus was here. If anybody ask you somethin' like that again, I want you to tell them that you don't know no Marcus. Okay?"

Linell and Latrell both agreed to what their older sister was saying before one headed to the kitchen the other back into the living room and in front of the television. There Kayla stood, in the dining room leaning on a chair at the dining room table. She had never felt fear strike like this in her body for one day in her life. At that very moment she realized that whoever had shot up Marcus' place earlier that day must know where she lived....

BCPL
Baltimore County
Public Library

CPSIA information can be obtained
at www.ICGtesting.com
Printed in the USA
LVOW10s2008140617
538120LV00018B/397/P